"**P**oor people are not young and carefree," Aretha growled. "We can't afford young and carefree, only rich people can buy young and carefree. And if you believe for one moment that I am going to allow you to screw up your life with Guy Wiley, the farmer, you have a next thing coming."

Lucia gasped. "How did Guy come into this?"

"Because he is the reason you aren't taking Ace Jackson seriously." Aretha huffed. "I get it, Guy is handsome and well-spoken and charming, and you have a crush, but he is a farmer, not a doctor. He is not going anywhere working the land on his uncle's farm. Besides, a man who looks like that is not going to be faithful to one woman."

THE PERFECT GUY

BRENDA BARRETT

JAMAICA TREASURES

The Perfect Guy

A Jamaica Treasures Book/August 2018

Published by Jamaica Treasures
Kingston, Jamaica

This is a work of fiction. Names, characters, places, and incidents are either the product of the author's imagination or are used fictitiously. Any resemblance to an actual person or persons, living or dead, events, or locales is entirely coincidental.

Jamaica Treasures
P.O. Box 482
Kingston 19
Jamaica W.I.
www.fiwibooks.com

ABOUT THE AUTHOR

Books have always been a big part of life for Jamaican born Brenda Barrett, she reports that she gets withdrawal symptoms if she does not consume at least two books per week. That is all she can manage these days, as her days are filled with writing, a natural progression from her love of reading. Currently, Brenda has several novels on the market, she writes predominantly in the historical fiction, Christian fiction, comedy and romance genres.

Apart from writing fictional books, Brenda writes for her blogs blackhair101.com; where she gives hair care tips and fiwibooks.com, where she shares about her writing life.

You can connect with Brenda online at:
Brenda-Barrett.com
Twitter.com/AuthorWriterBB
Facebook.com/AuthorBrendaBarrett

Prologue

"**H**er breasts are coming in." Craig whistled as the girl passed the road where they were installing a fence. "Who wants to bet that she will be mine by tomorrow?"

"Not betting," Ray, another laborer muttered. "The family is so dirt poor that her mother will be pimping her out in no time. The big brother came by here looking for work this morning. The poor thing was hungry. I gave him my lunch and the little bit of money I had on me. I told him we had enough people to do the fence. He couldn't work anyway; he looked skinny and hungry like he is malnourished."

"That's good to know that she is hungry." Craig sounded as if he were smacking his lips. "I can feed her all the food that she wants."

"Such a shame if she becomes one of your baby mothers," Ray grunted. "Because that girl is different. Very sweet personality and so pretty. All of that dark rich skin— almost luminous and that long curly hair. She is the kind of girl that would make a killing modeling on the world stage if given the opportunity. Definitely haven't seen anybody quite like her before."

"Yeah, she is pretty for a black girl," Craig said dismissively. "All my baby mothers are light skinned. She could be the exception."

"She is pretty, full stop," Ray grunted. "If I had the money, I would make sure that she doesn't fall into your clutches but I am a churchman now and waiting on the Lord for a wife.

"Besides, that girl is jailbait. She is too young to be in a relationship like the one you want. That's the problem with the men in this neighborhood; they have no concern for a girl's age."

That's when Guy looked up.

He had been half listening to the conversation between the two laborers while he worked out with the engineer how they would put proper drainage on the property.

He was on a mission to modernize his uncle Micky's thirty acres of farmland and make things much easier for the old man and himself.

The number one problem in the valleys was flooding, and Micky had lost nearly five acres of coffee plants in the last rains.

Guy heard Ray's end of the conversation with Craig.

He vaguely registered that they were talking about a girl. He had looked across at the men and then in the direction that Craig was leering.

And then he saw her and instantly forgot about the drainage systems, rock topography, and geology. It was as though something changed around and within him. He immediately felt protective.

He hadn't even seen her face. She had stopped and was looking down at her feet in what looked like the tattiest slippers he had ever seen. It had an indistinct color and looked like a dog had chewed around it.

"Who is she?" Guy turned to Craig and Ray.

"Her name is Lucia," Ray was the one who answered. "She has a brother named Earl and another one a little younger than her named Nate. The brother Earl is seventeen, she is just fifteen, and the younger brother is fourteen."

"Their mother, Aretha, just moved here from the poor house in Port Antonio. They are now living in Beatrice Mcbean's house."

"The cottage where the walls are practically falling apart?" Guy asked appalled. "That place is not habitable."

"They live there though," Ray sniffed. "The church has been helping them with food, and clothes and things since they came into the community, but that's not a regular thing. I doubt the children are even going to school."

Craig licked his lips. "I can help her with that."

"It's the family that needs help," Ray said in disgust beating Guy to it. "Not just the girl. She does not need your kind of help."

"You are going to leave this girl alone, Craig." Guy looked up the road where she was hopping in her half slipper, her long ponytail bouncing behind her.

"I saw her first." Craig protested.

"All you are going to do is look." Guy turned to Craig, "and tell your friends and everyone else that Lucia is not available. Hands off, or face the consequences."

"Which means no work in the district." Ray murmured for good measure. "Don't worry Guy; I will help spread the news. There are too many thirsty men around here who should know better."

"He wants her for himself," Craig sneered. "Why should I be the one who backs down, Guy Wiley is not God."

"How many children do you have, Craig?" Guy asked.

"What?" Craig shrugged. "Maybe nine. I wasn't named as the father for a few."

"Amazing," Ray murmured, "and he is not even twenty-five yet."

"How many girlfriends?" Guy looked at Craig assessingly.

"Just two at the moment." Craig bragged.

"And who provides for this harem?" Guy raised an eyebrow.

"I work for Micky," Craig spoke less than confidently now; he had never taken any thought to who his bosses were, the place was called Micky's Coffee Farm. Therefore, he assumed Micky was the boss.

"When last have you seen Micky on this coffee farm?" Guy asked.

"Well I," Craig looked down at the ground. "I don't know...I report to Jonesy, not you."

"And Jonesy reports to Guy," Ray said snidely. "You have no sense. Connect the dots."

Craig shrugged. "I can leave the girl alone."

"Good." Guy nodded, "her name is Lucia, you heard Ray say her name."

Craig nodded. "I am going to leave Lucia alone."

"Say it one more time with meaning." Ray laughed, "You can't trust this village ram. He thinks he is the country stud. He is not going to let Lucia slip away."

"I promise, I will leave her alone." Craig muttered, "I have too many mouths to feed to risk losing my job here for one girl."

Craig looked directly at Guy. "I swear, and I will tell everyone who dares to look at her to back away—far away."

"Now that's better," Guy nodded. "Much better."

****

"Tell me about the family that lives in Beatrice Mcbean's condemned house," Guy said to Myrtle as soon as he stepped into the kitchen at Micky's house.

Myrtle was preparing something that smelled so scrumptious Guy had to stop and inhale the air.

Myrtle looked at him and grinned. "So you saw the pretty girl with the long hair."

"Yes," Guy nodded, "and then I heard that she is living in the worst conditions a person could live in. They would be better off in a tent than that place. Any minute the concrete can collapse with them sleeping. Where on earth do they sleep anyway?"

Myrtle shook her head. "They throw a tarpaulin over one of the three walls left standing. It is pretty bad. A couple of us in the community help out when we can. I send food over there regularly, and others help but...it's bad.

"I heard that the mother was fleeing from her husband. She ended up here because she is a distant relative of Beatrice. The house was abandoned; Beatrice had no close relatives to claim it, so I guess that is why she is living there. As bad as it is, I think it is a safe haven. Aretha that is the name of the mother said it was better than the poor house. That's where they were living."

"I see." Guy nodded.

"Aretha is a hard worker and could do with a job." Myrtle shook her head, "A little birdie told me that she had an affair with Chilton Wray, from Wray Hardware and got pregnant for him and that resulted in the girl Lucia."

"Chilton Wray is married."

"And so was Aretha." Myrtle snorted. "That is part of the problem I guess. I heard the husband tried to kill her."

Guy leaned on the counter and watched as Myrtle chopped up carrots like a professional chef.

"The mother is in her thirties and still pretty young. I think she got a hard knock in life to be living this way. That's why I asked Lillie from the basic school to hire her as a custodian. Their last person left the other day."

"I want to help too, surely the custodian pay is just a pittance," Guy murmured, "But I have to do it anonymously. I don't want to be considered some kind of benefactor that they'll be beholden to in the future."

"You are such a good boy." Myrtle looked at him, her eyes crinkling in the corners as she smiled.

"I am twenty-two, Myrtle," Guy shook his head, "far from a boy."

"Ha," Myrtle chortled. "Twenty-two looks like an infant when you are forty years older. How are you going to help anonymously?"

"I'll think of something," Guy said moving away from the counter. "One thing is for sure, I have to get them out of that building soon. Do you know if Wayne is free?"

"The builder, Wayne?" Myrtle widened her eyes. "Guy, you are not going to build a house for them?"

"Yes." Guy nodded. "Just a three bedroom cottage. Simple design. I want Lucia to have her own room; her mother can have her own and the boys share. They need electricity and running water, and all three of them are going to school in the next term.

"I am taking that on. I am going to have to arrange for Dominic Black our manager at the Wiley Groceries in Port Antonio to send them groceries every week, and I need to get clothes and shoes for them all. You are going to have to get the measurements."

"Can you afford it?" Myrtle frowned, "you recently left college, your business is just getting on its feet, you just took on Micky's coffee farm wholeheartedly, and you are going to Canada to do your masters."

"I can afford it," Guy shrugged, "I have shares in the family business. We make money; we have quite a few supermarkets now. I get a yearly dividend, which is quite hefty. Besides, I haven't spent a dime of the money I get from the coffee farm. And it does make money, especially since I took over years ago.

"Micky's heart wasn't in it, and he was too old-fashioned in his approach to make much. I am running a professional outfit now. When I go overseas I am leaving Horace Jones in charge here. My foreman Ron Getty will be in charge of the strawberry farm. They are good honest men."

"But you are investing so much in people you do not even know." Myrtle protested. "Why?"

Guy contemplated the question for a while, long enough for Myrtle to start prepping a platter of fish for roasting in her outdoor brick oven.

The hefty fish were caught in the river below the house. They were practically fresh, just recently scaled.

She had quite forgotten about the question by the time he answered.

"Maybe because it is the right thing to do. You and other community people do what you can. I have the means to do much more," Guy said finally.

Myrtle looked at him and chuckled. "Or maybe because you like that girl and you are willing to do anything for her, there is no shame in admitting your motives."

Guy shook his head. "You were the one who pointed out that I don't know them. Besides, I doubt she will ever know that I am behind all this because I just thought of a charity name that will help them anonymously, the Farm Help Society. What do you think about that?"

Myrtle frowned. "Farm Help Society? Sounds good.

Sounds large, like a big committee of charitable folks."

Myrtle chuckled. "The FHS, it has a very legit sound to it."

"I am happy you like it." Guy smiled, "because you are going to be the face of it. And you will be in charge while I am gone."

****

It took Guy three months to turn around the misfortunes of the family completely. In that time he had gotten to know them better. He had volunteered to work on the house with Wayne and his men. Just so that he could keep an eye on the progress of the building.

Aretha he realized was a fierce mother hen. She was still quite attractive, she was the object of Wayne's flirtation for the duration of the job, but she knew how to hold her own.

"You know who she reminds me of? Erykah Badu, the singer," Wayne would repeat like a broken record.

"Every time she steps out of the house I feel like she is going to tell me, '*You better call Tyrone, tell him I said to come home and pack your stuff.*'"

That was usually greeted with laughter.

Aretha did have more than a passing resemblance to Erykah Badu. She had a lighter complexion than the singer though, and she kept her hair in a fade cut. He didn't know if it was intentioned, but her hairstyle emphasized her eyes, which were a liquid rich brown, almost the exact match of dark chocolate liqueur. Thick short eyelashes surrounded her eyes; it made for a striking combination.

He had initially thought she had on thick mascara, but she had passed on the distinct eye color and the thick eyelashes to all her children.

On Lucia, it took on greater depth. She had a darker skin

tone than her relatives and corkscrew curls that reached down her back. Her mahogany skin tone emphasized the whiteness of her eyes and her whiter than white teeth.

Her lips were so deep red they were almost black. Lucia was magnetic to look at. Once she appeared in the vicinity, it was hard to look away.

The men were careful to pretend as if Lucia did not exist, though she was hard to ignore. Whenever she came outside, a polite silence descended among them.

He had warned them off, and they took heed, except for one laborer who had whispered quite loudly for him to hear.

"That girl is going to be drop-dead gorgeous one day."

"That day is today," another brave soul whispered.

He silently agreed. Though he had glared a warning at the speaker.

They had finished a bedroom, bathroom, the open area living room and kitchen in record time. Lucia had walked out of the house, excitement in her eyes, searching for him among the men.

Guy walked toward her, his boots muddied, his shirt splattered with cement. It occurred to him while walking toward her that he could almost feel an invisible pull. It happened the first time they met, and it persisted even now.

"Guy! My birthday is not for another month. She waved the card he had left with the gift on their newly finished veranda. "Did you really give me this for my birthday? A camera?"

Her eyes widened in awe.

Guy nodded. Her birthday was the end of August. He was going to be in Canada by then. He had an all expenses paid scholarship, to do his Masters in plant science at the University of British Colombia.

"You said you wanted to capture memories, that's a good

way to do it."

"Thank you," Lucia squealed, hugging him tight to her, ignoring his cement splattered shirt.

She hugged him for too long, relaxing in his arms. The silence around them was deafening as the men observed their interaction.

Guy reminded himself once again that she was still just a girl. A very pretty teenage girl, on the cusp of womanhood, but still just a girl.

His hands-off speeches were meant for himself as well. At twenty-two, to her fifteen years they were seven years apart in not just age and experience but maturity. He was her self-designated protector. He wanted to preserve her innocence for as long as was possible.

All his feelings toward her were placed in dormancy, put on ice.

He was going to wait until she grew up. He was patient like that. It was a character trait that farming had honed to perfection.

He put his arm around her, gave her a little squeeze and stepped back from her embrace.

All his noble speeches to himself couldn't downplay the fact that he was a man and she was a desirable female. He was almost happy that he wouldn't be seeing her for a year.

Chapter One

Five and a half years later

"Stop talking to Guy Wiley. Stop entertaining him. Stop mooning over him. He is good looking yes, nobody can deny that, but he is as poor as a church mouse."

Lucia glared at her mother. She was not mooning over Guy Wiley. So she had been caught looking at a picture that she had taken of him when he was in his uncle Micky's field. He had been shirtless and posed with his hand on a hoe and looking out in the distance. It was a beautiful photo. It showed the raw beauty of the valleys and its subject was a man who did not look like the stereotypical farmer.

Her mother would not see the loveliness of the composition or the vividness of the colors. Her mother saw things in black and white, money or no money, rich or poor, farmer or doctor.

For her mother taking pictures was a pointless hobby and talking to Guy Wiley, the only person in her life who seemed to understand her, was meaningless. They had been too poor for too long for her to be flirting with the idea of pretty pictures and even prettier men.

Her mother wanted her to marry the doctor. She said it more than ten times a day and doubled that on the weekends.

And she was about to lecture her about it now. Lucia looked at her and put away the pictures. She figured that now would not be a good time to tell her mom that she had gotten a wedding gig.

A paying gig, to take the pictures for a relative of a coworker at the supermarket where she worked.

Chad had seen some of her pictures, showed it to his sister and now she was hired. The only problem was that the wedding was in Kingston and she needed some more equipment to really wow the crowd with her photography skills.

Her savings account had in enough money so the bank would not close the thing and her next four paychecks were already budgeted. However, the roof on the three-bedroom cottage needed fixing.

The roof was a sieve. Every time the rain fell they had to find additional buckets to place at strategic locations throughout the house. It had drizzled today, and there was a staccato drip drip sound that could be heard like an off-key choir.

It could be worse, Lucia supposed. A few years ago they had no floor or even roof. They had thrown a tarpaulin over the bare concrete walls when it rained.

Those were lean years. She and her brothers barely survived it. They had even lived at the poorhouse once; it had been a better experience than where they were in Norridge where her mother's husband, Keith had almost killed them in a house fire.

And then someone had mentioned to her mother that her distant relative had died leaving a house in the valleys. Her mother had packed them up, and they had moved anticipating a house of their own only to find a one-room shed with collapsed concrete walls.

They were still grateful; living in a poorhouse had negative connotations. She and her two brothers were mercilessly teased when they were in that situation.

Besides, living in the valley was like living among extended family, the valley residents were extremely kind. The community at Bowden Pen had some of the warmest people in the world.

Not to mention the charitable organization, the Farm Help Society that had basically carried them through the last five years. It was as if that particular charity was looking out for her family exclusively. Everything she owned, even the clothes on her back was from the charity.

They had been religiously delivering groceries and toiletries to them every week. And in December, Lucia, her mom, and brothers got a full wardrobe. And they were not second-hand clothes. Whoever shopped for them knew them and knew what they liked. The Farm Help Society had even built them a proper dwelling. She wondered if she should ask them to fix the roof. She didn't want to be a burden, but if they could help, she could take out a loan, buy a proper camera lens, maybe a camera stand or two, as well as a smaller camera than her Nikon D700...

"Lucia!" her mother had been talking, but she had not heard a word. "Are you listening to me?"

"No ma'am," Lucia said truthfully. "I was er... thinking I should write the Farm Help Society and ask for help with the roof."

"Say what now?" Her mother growled. "You never heard a word I just said did you? I already told Dr. Jackson and he said he would fix the roof."

"In exchange for what?" Lucia raised an eyebrow.

"You are not a dumb person. The man likes you. You could at least pretend to be interested. He is a doctor!" Aretha shook her head. "Do you have any idea what that means? What it could mean for you and us?"

It was not a question that required an answer and Lucia restrained herself from giving a snarky reply. Her mother was borderline abusive and would probably strangle her where she sat if she said anything even remotely negative about her precious, Dr. Ace Jackson.

Her mother discussed him with the kind of reverence that suggested that he was not just a mere doctor but deity.

It had gotten worse since she started working for him and had the lofty title of 'housekeeper.' It was her best paying job in years.

Lucia wished she could be happier for her mother, but she had the uncomfortable sensation that her mother only got to keep the job because of Ace's interest in her. He had not wanted a permanent housekeeper until he met her in his driveway a year ago.

What would happen to her mother's job if she rejected him?

She got up from the sofa and stretched. "Do you want me to start dinner or will you?"

"I took dinner from Dr. Jackson's house." Aretha hated the change of topic. She had been poised to give Lucia another long lecture.

She didn't understand how her daughter was acting so nonchalant about the doctor. Lucia did not have the right priorities. All the girl did was talk about cameras and photographs and Guy Wiley.

If she were Lucia's age and had her looks, she would be all over Ace Jackson like a skin rash.

Ace had moved into the community a full year now but had taken an interest in Lucia the minute he first saw her.

Who wouldn't?

Aretha eyed her daughter as she strode over to their kitchen and pulled the covers off the plastic dishes inspecting the food.

Lucia was an attractive girl; facially she was perfect, she had inherited all the best features from Aretha and the deadbeat sperm donor father who still pretended as if she did not exist.

Lucia had been a pretty baby. She had looked like a little doll, like a little chocolate drop with a mop of curls.

Aretha inhaled deeply and then sat in the chair that Lucia had occupied.

Lucia had been the result of a six months affair with Chilton Wray, her married boss when she was working at his hardware store in Port Antonio.

It was the stupidest thing she had ever done. It was on the top of her list of regrets in life, that and the fact that she had cheated on her very hardworking, mild-mannered husband who had been away on the farm-working program in America.

When Keith returned, she had been four months pregnant with Chilton's baby. It had broken Keith's heart, sent him to drink, changed his personality, turned him into an abusive monster.

He had kicked her from the house and kept Earl who was one year old at the time. To add to her unfortunate situation, Chilton had denied being the father and fired her at the insistence of his wife.

She had hit rock bottom, pregnant, and alone with no place to live. The community knew what she had done and was squarely on her husband's side. She was rejected from all sides.

It was all her fault and she accepted it.

She had to move back in with her parents who were so poor they had been on government assistance. That was when she had resorted to begging in Port Antonio square for help with her pregnancy.

Keith had seen her one day looking pathetic and hungry and very pregnant and had asked her to come back home. He hadn't quite forgiven her; it was more a matter of convenience. He had to go back to the States to work and had nobody to leave Earl with.

She had Lucia after that episode. She had vowed that her precious daughter's life would be different. None of her mistakes would taint her child.

Unfortunately, the years had not gone so well. They had moved from poor to below poor. Keith had returned to Jamaica when Lucia was around six months old. He had confessed that he couldn't bear to look at the baby.

Lucia had a dark nutmeg color, and her hair was a mop of silky loose curls. She was obviously Chilton Wray's child. It was as if God had given her a child so that all the world could see her indiscretion.

Keith ignored the baby, pretended that she didn't exist. It was his way to cope, and Aretha understood that.

Once she didn't mention Lucia or picked her up when she cried or paid any undue attention to the baby while he was home everything was fine. It brought peace to the house and quelled Keith's rage.

When she got pregnant again a year and a few months later with Nate, Keith went back to being unhinged.

Unfortunately, Nate did not resemble his father, he took after her side of the family, and Keith became suspicious of her afresh.

Keith was a biracial man with olive toned skin and freckles. Earl looked very much like his father but Nate did not.

No reassurance that she had not cheated could quell his speculation. No argument could soothe his rage. She had insisted on her innocence pleaded with him to think about it, black people came in all different shades with different hair types.

But Keith didn't listen. He went around the neighborhood asking people who slept with his wife.

People discussed it on the shop piazzas. They compared all the men in the village with Nate trying to find matching features.

She had become a spectacle, the village laughing stock once more. Her husband was hurt, and he wanted the whole world to know it.

Aretha had to leave the marital home again, this time even her parents didn't want to have anything to do with her.

For years she lived with her three children in a one-room board hovel on her parents' property. Her father had stopped speaking to her altogether, and her mother had grudgingly helped out with food when the children were starving. She frequently had to leave her toddlers alone in the house while she worked.

She had taken up two jobs to survive, but with three children under five, it had been tough going.

And then it got worse, much worse. A troublemaker from the community told Keith that their son, Earl, was his and not Keith's.

It had been a lie. Earl was very much Keith's, he was his carbon copy, but Keith had been drunk at the time and fuelled with rage.

He had found them in the scrap of a house and had been angry enough to try to burn them alive one night, all four of them. He didn't care anymore; he had wanted revenge for her unfaithfulness.

After their stint in the poor house and moving to the Upper Rio Grande Valley's Aretha had learned her lesson.

She had one daughter, and she was pretty, Lucia was not going to have the kind of life that she had. Not over her dead body. As far as she was concerned, they had hit the jackpot with the doctor. He liked Lucia, was practically obsessed with her from the moment he had seen her.

To Aretha, it was a blessing.

They had been charity cases for years from a very generous charity, but it was time for them to step up and cross over the poverty line. Lucia was the key to that.

Aretha sighed loudly.

Lucia looked up from sharing out her food and frowned. "What's wrong?"

"Nothing." Aretha got up. "I was just thinking that I want you to have a better life than I have had so far."

"Me too." Lucia nodded, "that's why I am working on the photography thing. I think I can make a go of this, Mom. Can you believe that in, a couple of hours, I can make the equivalent of what I earn in one month working at the supermarket? It's crazy!"

Aretha scowled. "Can you believe that in one day you can marry Dr. Jackson and be set for life? Where is your ambition?"

Lucia looked down at her plate and heaved a sigh. "Can I eat my dinner in peace?"

Aretha ignored her. "What is wrong with Ace Jackson? Tell me, what fault do you find with this man?"

"Nothing, he is lovely, perfect," Lucia mumbled. "It's just that I want to have a career in photography and I wouldn't mind marrying for love rather than money."

"You are watching too many television shows and reading too many fairy tales," Aretha snorted.

"But Earl has a job," Lucia sighed, she had lost her appetite. She felt as if her mother was turning the screws too tightly; she had that determined glint in her eye.

"And Nate is at university. I only want a chance to live my life the way that I want. I want to have a career, and if I marry, I want it to be for love..." *and to Guy Wiley*, though she wouldn't say that out loud.

She didn't have room in her heart for anyone else. Guy was well and truly entrenched there.

"Poor people are not young and carefree," Aretha growled. "We can't afford young and carefree, only rich people can buy young and carefree. And if you believe for one moment that I am going to allow you to screw up your life with Guy Wiley, the farmer, you have a next thing coming."

Lucia gasped. "How did Guy come into this?"

"Because he is the reason you aren't taking Ace Jackson seriously." Aretha huffed. "I get it, Guy is handsome and well-spoken and charming, and you have a crush, but he is a farmer, not a doctor. He is not going anywhere working the land on his uncle's farm. Besides, a man who looks like that is not going to be faithful to one woman."

"Guy is not a womanizer!" Lucia couldn't resist shouting.

"How would you know?" Aretha frowned, "he only comes up here every two weeks or so. You have no clue what he is doing elsewhere."

"He works on a strawberry farm in St. Andrew." Lucia hissed. "He works hard and yet he finds the time to come here to help out his uncle Micky and to see me."

"Lord give me strength," Aretha mumbled. "Strength lord. Strength. This stubborn mule of a child is going to kill me."

"It's not right, targeting Ace for marriage just because you want to live better," Lucia said fiercely. "There is value in working hard for your own money!"

"Where did you get that from?" Aretha snarled, "poor farmer Guy who drives an ugly rusty vehicle that you can hear from a mile away? Poor farmer Guy who doesn't even have a skill other than farming? Can he even read? Girl, you are going to have some ambition, or I am going to slap some into you! I am not letting any pretty face man turn you into an idiot!"

There was a knock on the door before Lucia could rebut.

Aretha glared at her, a warning in her eyes. "I will deal with you later."

She wiped her palms on her skirt and then opened the door.

Ace smiled widely. "Did somebody request fixing the roof?"

Lucia's heart stilled. Had he heard any of the conversation? They hadn't exactly been whispering. Did he know that her mother had her eyes on him like he was some savior and prize?

"Ooh Dr. Jackson," her mother had on her 'suck up' voice, "I had no idea you were coming over to fix the roof yourself."

"God forbid, no. I am not exactly the handiest of men," Ace laughed, "I brought the workmen with me."

He glanced around her mother and looked at her. "Hey, Lucia."

"Hey, Ace." Lucia waved her fork at him.

Her mother glared at her for her casual attitude. "Why don't you go outside and talk with Dr. Jackson, Lucia."

"I'd like that." Ace smiled at her, "we can go into Port

Antonio and get something to eat."

Lucia looked down at the food in her hand reluctantly. "But, I already have..."

"Carry it for lunch tomorrow at work." Aretha cut in before she could protest further.

And moving faster than she thought she was capable of Aretha reached where Lucia was standing in the kitchenette and took the food from her.

"Maybe you should go and put on a nicer dress," she whispered.

Ace heard. "No, she is fine. I was thinking of going to KFC. Nothing fancy."

Aretha all but pushed her through the door.

Chapter Two

Guy rubbed his eyes for the fourth time. He had the kind of day that he was thankful was coming to an end. Usually, he wouldn't have driven so far to get to Port Antonio on a Wednesday, but he had a business meeting with his farm manager at his recent acquisition, a mango farm in St. Ann's Bay.

They had discussed his plans for the place, and then he had taken the hour and a half drive to Port Antonio on a whim. He could stay at his villa tonight and then visit Bowden Pen tomorrow.

So that he could check up on Micky and Myrtle and see Lucia of course. He would have to change vehicles though. His Ranger Rover was too showy and would interfere with his experiment with Lucia.

He could borrow Pastor Tate's green pick up. It wasn't nearly as battered looking like his old Betsy, but it was far from fancy.

He stopped at the gas station adjacent to the KFC store and had to rub his eyes again, this time in disbelief. He could clearly see Lucia getting out of a black Pajero; she was with the doctor, Ace Jackson.

He was saying something to her, and she was laughing. They looked happy together. Guy inhaled raggedly.

Suddenly he wasn't feeling as weary as he was before, white-hot jealousy coursed through him, acting like several cups of coffee on his tiredness.

The gas attendant came to his window, and he didn't acknowledge him for a full minute. He watched in frozen disbelief as Lucia and Ace walked into KFC together.

Ace was semi-formally dressed in a buttoned-up short sleeve shirt. He held the door open, and Lucia glided through smiling at him. She was in a yellow floral dress that fit her perfectly. It hugged her curves in all the right places. Her hair bounced behind her in a profusion of curls as she swished her hips all the way up to the cashier.

Guy curled his fingers around the steering wheel. He gritted his teeth when Ace casually put his hand in the small of her back. He read that as an intimate gesture of togetherness.

"Sir, how much gas do you want?" The attendant asked patiently.

Guy looked at the man in confusion; he had almost forgotten where he was.

"Fill her up." He looked at his gas gage and then back at the attendant apologetically, "I'll say when."

He got his gas and then contemplated what to do. Should he spy on them? Somehow that felt like a rotten thing to do. Wasn't he the one who had convinced himself that he would wait until Lucia chose him for who he was?

He drove over to KFC and parked beside Ace Jackson. His car windows were tinted, they wouldn't be able to see him especially as it got darker but he could see them clearly as they took a seat near the window with their orders.

He knew what Lucia would be having. He had been the first one to introduce her to fast food. She had never been to a restaurant before he took her on her seventeenth birthday.

That was nearly four years ago. Four!

Had he waited too long for Lucia to grow up?

He felt a low thrumming in his head, and he rubbed his temple. He knew about Ace's interest in her. He knew that her mother thought the sun rose and set on the doctor. Had he waited too long?

He slid down into the car seat and observed every laugh, every gesture like a person watching an accident about to happen but was helpless to do anything about it.

Except he wasn't helpless, he could waltz into the place now and declare to Lucia, I am the Farm Help Society. That mystical organization that has built your home, put food on your table, sent you and your brothers to school and even taken care of your mother.

And after that what? She would gasp in gratitude and hug him, and they would drive off into the sunset and live happily ever after.

He doubted that.

He never wanted Lucia to be with him out of a sense of duty or gratitude. Besides, he had always found it a bit sleazy to help because he wanted something in return.

His intentions toward her were pure, he had seen a need, and he wanted her to have as normal of a life as possible.

Unfortunately, normalcy came with competition for her affections. Just this last year when he had decided to start taking a more serious tone with Lucia, Ace walked in. Ace Jackson who had no qualms about pulling out all the stops to impress her with his wealth.

Guy knew that this could have happened, but somehow he had never anticipated such a formidable competitor such as Ace.

Ace was a young man, just four years older than he was which made him thirty-two years old.

He was single, polite, went to church regularly, and was from a close-knit family. Ace had no debts, had no bad relationships in his past or strange proclivities. He was squeaky clean according to the investigative report that Guy had requested on him.

Ace ran a private practice in Port Antonio which had previously belonged to his father, Ace Jackson senior, and he lived in the unspoiled and relaxed atmosphere of the valleys in the house where he was born.

How could Guy have anticipated that competition of Ace's caliber would move into the Upper Rio Grande Valleys?

The local men he could warn off, a doctor who had no issues, was another creature altogether.

Who could blame Ace Jackson for seeing Lucia and liking her? Lucia was exceptional to look at. Added to that, she had a sunny personality and an open nature that would be attractive to anyone.

And most importantly unlike most of the girls in the district, she was unencumbered by two or three babies at her age.

He had until now kept things casual. He had no idea if that was the right thing to do because lately he had driven way past like and was currently under the throes of what he was interpreting as love.

Guy winced when Ace moved closer to Lucia and pulled a curl and tucked it behind her ear.

If he wanted to sleep tonight and to keep his sanity he had to get out of here. Lucia had no obligation to him. He had never wanted his acts of kindness to her and her family to instill any hero worship or obligation.

He started the car and drove out of the parking lot. If Lucia was going to love him, it was going to be as Guy, without strings attached.

And if she chose the doctor?

Guy couldn't think about that right now but based on his current jealousy he knew he wouldn't be particularly happy.

Chapter Three

Ace was in the middle of a story about his family when Lucia looked through the window.

She had the disconcerting sensation that Guy was near. She liked to call it her Guy-sense. It had been fine-tuned over the years.

She looked out at the parking lot eagerly but didn't see him. Guy's vehicle was a distinct shade of rust. It was mostly green on one side, but the rest of it was brown. It could be heard from a mile away, so he wasn't in the vicinity.

And then her eyes got pulled to a Range Rover; it was dark gray.

Her older brother, Earl, was car mad and he had always fantasized about having a vehicle like it.

She looked at the Range contemplatively. The vehicle was tinted, but the front was clear enough. Someone was sitting in it.

Maybe a man? Maybe Guy?

Nobody else looked like Guy, not in Portland. Maybe not in the entire world. It had to be him. She watched as the vehicle pulled out of the parking lot.

What would he be doing in such a high-end vehicle? And had he seen her with Ace?

It was never spoken between them, but she knew that Guy thought she was special. Sometimes he came to the valleys to see her. Like that time it rained like crazy, and the Matthews Bridge collapsed, and nobody could enter or leave the community. Guy had come across by boat just to see if she was okay.

Would he be mad that she was here with Ace? She had no clue. The thing about Guy, she never really knew where she stood with him. Was he just a friend? Or did he want them to be something more?

One thing was for sure, his intentions toward her were not apparent. He wasn't like the rest of men in her neighborhood who whistled at her or called her princess. One man had even told her he would sell the boat that he used to make a living just for one night with her.

Even Ace showed his interest. He wasn't hiding it. She knew where she stood with him. He kept a respectful distance but he flirted with her and took her to KFC, and he fixed her roof all with one thing in mind. He was making his intentions clear.

Guy was different. If he had fixed the roof or taken her to KFC, she would have just thought that was Guy being friendly. Guy took her younger brother Nate to KFC as well, and he sometimes drove about with Earl. He was the one who had taught Earl to drive.

Guy was a family friend.

A family friend that she had the hugest thing for...

"What's wrong?" Ace asked snapping Lucia out of her

thoughts.

He sensed that he had lost her attention.

Lucia looked at him guiltily. "Nothing is wrong. I just thought I saw Guy."

"The farmer?" Ace looked behind him. "Where?"

"Driving that Range Rover," Lucia shrugged, "I must have been wrong."

"You must be mistaken," Ace murmured. "What would Guy Wiley be doing in a vehicle like that, I can't even afford a Range Rover."

Lucia changed the subject hurriedly. She had no intention of speaking about finances or who could afford what. She definitely didn't want Guy to be the topic of discussion.

Ace moved to the valleys when they weren't as bad as they used to be. They were mostly normal now thanks to the Farm Help Society, but they weren't always like that.

As a matter of fact, she vividly remembered when Ace moved to the valleys. She had helped her mother to air out and clean up the plantation style house where he lived. Her mother had been over the moon happy that she had gotten the job as the temporary housekeeper in one of the better houses in Bowden Pen.

Situated on a hill, with its white columns and airy verandas with a view of the Rio Grande it was easy to feel like a lady of the manor when standing on the staircase or gliding through the passageways with the gleaming hardwood floors.

The construction crew had refreshed the place with paint and fixed boards and made it look new. Lucia and Aretha had made it smell like new by giving the inside a thorough cleaning; that was ten years overdue.

Micky Wiley had been in the garden doing his best to make the terraced gardens look less unruly, Lucia was collecting lemons from him to make lemonade when the car had driven up, and Ace had stepped out.

He didn't look like what she had pictured in her head. In her head, doctors were grumpy old men that smelled like cough syrup. But Ace Jackson was tall, leanly muscular, his hair cut in a Mohawk style and he was young.

He looked like he was in his twenties.

"Good-looking fellow." Micky had declared with pride while Ace had walked up to the house and inspected the renovations.

Lucia could remember nodding. "He is too young to be a doctor."

"That boy is thirty-one years old," Micky murmured, "I was working here the day he was born. I remember the date and time when his mother showed up at the top of the walkway and hollered, "Help me I am going to have this baby!"

Lucia chuckled. "Did you help her?"

"No," Micky frowned, "I ran for Myrtle who was at the back and then they carried her inside. That was women's work. I stayed outside and got the good news. It was a proud moment. Look at him now."

Lucia had walked up with lemons in hand and Ace had turned to her and stood still. "Am I imagining you?"

"Who, me?" Lucia had asked curiously.

"Yes," Ace had smiled, and she had thought how his smile transformed him into a very handsome man. He had walked up to her and pinched her.

"Ouch." Lucia rubbed her arm. "What's wrong with you?"

"Just checking that you are real. Who are you?"

"Lucia Wray, your temporary housekeeper's daughter."

"Lucia means graceful light." Ace had looked at her with overt interest. "St Lucia was a virgin martyr who died in the 4th century. Her name was invoked against eye disease."

Lucia frowned. "Eye disease?"

"Yep." Ace smiled again. "Ironic huh, because I couldn't believe my eyes when I saw you."

She had nodded awkwardly and then mumbled something about lemonade.

Ace had thoughtfully watched her as she went inside.

Since then their interactions had been mostly brief and slightly uncomfortable for her until recently.

He was finding more and more ways for them to interact and her mother wholeheartedly encouraged it.

Since then she had found out that Ace had a great personality. It was common knowledge, but she was just catching on.

In less than a year after taking over Dr. Garvey's practice, he was pretty popular in the town and the district.

His youth belied his knowledge. He was even considered better than Dr. Garvey who had been everybody's favorite general practitioner.

"Earth to Lucia," Ace said waving a finger in front of her, "you zoned out for a minute there."

"I guess I did," Lucia smiled and looked down into her box of hot wings. "I was wondering why did you come here to practice? It's not exactly glamorous."

"Here, as in Port Antonio?" Ace raised a brow, "my father refuses to come back, he says he is too busy. I am the eldest child and a fellow GP, so I was charged with the task of wrapping up his practice with Garvey, they never dissolved their partnership and Garvey was retiring.

"And then I was tasked with selling the family house in the valleys. I have several interested persons who want the house, no serious offers yet. Most of them want to turn it into a guesthouse or bed and breakfast."

Lucia nodded. "It's a nice place."

"That's where I grew up until we moved to Kingston."

"I didn't know you grew up there," Lucia said. "Micky said you were born there. I thought you just liked the countryside that's why you were staying there for the time being."

"I do like it." Ace shook his head. "I had no intentions of staying so long and even practicing here for so long. I just came back to sell the house and the practice. If you had asked me several years ago if I saw myself in rural Jamaica at this point, I would have said no."

Lucia nodded. "Rural life is not for everyone."

"I thought so too when I got here," Ace sighed. "The slower pace was about to drive me crazy, but Garvey begged me to stay a while to see to his patients. He was pretty persuasive.

"But I can't credit me staying to just him, the valley sunrises and a particular pretty girl contributed to me sticking around. So after one year, here I am."

"Why did you become a doctor?" Lucia asked changing the subject. She knew he was talking about her and she didn't want to get into that.

She had mixed feelings about Ace. To someone else, he would be perfect. To someone else, he would be an answer to prayers, but she felt something was missing.

The chemistry that she felt with Guy was missing with Ace. And maybe chemistry was only supposed to be felt between one person at a time, or maybe if her mother didn't try to ram him down her throat, she would actually feel something more for him.

"I became a doctor because it's the family business," Ace grinned, "all my siblings are doctors, Deuce is a pediatrician, Trey is an orthodontist."

"Your brothers are really named Deuce and Trey?" Lucia grinned. "Ace is one, and Deuce is two and Trey is three?"

"My mother is an avid poker player." Ace smiled wryly. " I

realized that you changed the subject, Lucia. I like you. You have to know that, right?

"Like, it is too mild a word for what I am feeling for you. I am not one to put my feelings out there, but there it is."

"Ace I..." Lucia swallowed.

"No pressure Lucia, I am a patient man," Ace said solemnly. "Have you heard the Bob Marley quote: "If she's amazing, she won't be easy. If she's easy, she won't be amazing. If she's worth it, you won't give up. If you give up, you're not worthy. ...

"I want to be worthy Lucia. I know that you are young and you are ambitious, and you want to make your own path. I understand that and I won't stifle you. I just want to be with you. I am ready to settle down, and I choose you."

"But I..." Lucia swallowed, "did my mother put you up to this? You overheard her this evening didn't you?"

"Yes," Ace nodded. "And no, she didn't put me up to this. Mother's have been pushing their daughters at me since I was a teenager. Your mother is quite persistent, but I understand where she is coming from. I am financially stable, and I am in a solid profession. Mothers like when their daughters marry doctors."

Lucia shook her head. "It's just thirsty and desperate."

Ace wove his hand into hers and squeezed. "And that my lady is but one of the reasons why I find you so attractive."

Chapter Four

Lucia struggled to wake up the next morning. It was the smell of plantains frying and loud chewing that dragged her out of a dream where a group of people was chasing her with sticks.

The dream had started nearly a year ago. Her mother's dream book said that her subconscious was avoiding an issue or a person.

It was no big mystery guessing what issue she was running from.

She opened her eyes slowly and saw Earl sitting on the lone chair in the corner of her room. He was eating an egg sandwich with unnecessary loudness.

Lucia groaned. "You chew louder than Miss Clem's pigs."

Earl grinned. "Morning to you too Sunshine."

Lucia glanced through the window, it was drizzling. Morning rain was a Portland thing.

"Sunshine, no way, I feel too cloudy for that. Welcome

home piggy."

Earl quirked a brow at her. "You sound grumpy. The way Mama has been carry on, I thought you would be up early and smelling the roses and singing with the birds."

"Mama is something else," Lucia murmured. "I went to KFC with Ace yesterday, and now she hears wedding bells."

Earl grinned. "When I walked in this morning, it was the first thing I heard...praises for the esteemed doctor."

"It is annoying." Lucia cracked an eye open and looked at her brother with more awareness. He had been away in Kingston for six months training to be a refrigerator electrician.

"How was the training?"

"Great." Earl took the last bite of his sandwich and then chewed it contemplatively.

Lucia watched him with a smile. He was tall and wiry. Her brother had tried everything to gain weight. He seemed as if he had finally succeeded; he had some definition in his arms.

He was boyishly handsome and still had that youthful look that said thirteen rather than twenty-one. He was growing a beard to add maturity to his features, but it wasn't quite working.

He still looked young, much younger than his age.

"I have my certificate," Earl said after he swallowed. "Showed it to Mama. She was praising Jesus and the Farm Help Society for the opportunity to make her family prosper. I am surprised her loud carrying on didn't wake you up."

Lucia grinned. "If I were awake, I would have joined her. I am happy for you E."

"You will be happier to hear that I got a job with the Cold Storage Company in St. Ann."

"St. Ann." Lucia whispered, "really?"

"Yup." Earl nodded, "they work with some major hotels,

maintaining and servicing their storage equipment. I didn't even finish the last class before the instructor recommended me."

"That's great," Lucia whispered, "but you are leaving me alone with Mama the rabid matchmaker."

Earl chuckled. "Being annoyed into marrying a doctor has never killed anybody. Wait until you hear about the pay. I am going to be set. At least until I am hired permanently. I will be on three months probation. I have to get on the job training and all of that.

"I also get a company vehicle which means I can visit you guys on my weekends off."

"That's cool," Lucia said her eyes glowing.

"By the way, I wrote to the Farm Help Society last week, gave the letter to Myrtle. I told them thank you for their assistance through the years, but we are at a point now where we can manage on our own. I will send some money every two weeks to help out with the expenses here. It's time we stand on our own feet."

"That's true." Lucia smiled. "And it is only fair that we stop depending on the Farm Help Society. Though I was thinking of asking for a camera lens."

Lucia sighed, "I got a wedding gig. An honest to goodness paying gig."

"Congrats," Earl smiled, his dimples deepened, making him appear impish. That only happened when Earl was genuinely pleased.

Lucia sat up in the bed and stretched. Her brother got it. He wasn't as dismissive of her talents as their mother, whose only end goal for her was somebody else taking care of her.

"It is time for the Farm Help Society to help another family," Earl said sternly, "I can help you with the lens after my work probation is up."

"It will be too late, the wedding is in two months," Lucia sighed. "And we are not exactly out of the woods, the roof is worse than ever, you know Ace brought some men to fix it yesterday."

"Well, they didn't do a good job. The roof is still leaking," Earl muttered, "I had to put several pails in the hall just this morning to catch the drips."

"Oh," Lucia rounded her eyes, "that sucks."

"I hope the doctor didn't pay those men." Earl rubbed his sparse beard. "I wish you had told me that the roof had gotten worse."

"You were in school," Lucia muttered, "no need to burden you with little problems."

"Those leaks out there are not little problems." Earl stood up. "It might have to be changed altogether. I'll have to ask Guy to help me with it. Guy is quite handy with these things. We fixed Micky's roof together a couple of years ago.

"If Guy was around when Wayne was putting on the roof, it would not be this bad. I think he used substandard materials. Wayne probably bought the cheapest materials he could find and then pocketed the rest of the money. All the roofs, he has done in the valleys do not last for more than a five years."

"Guy?" Lucia widened her eyes. "He is here in the valleys? Today?"

"Yes, got a ride from him this morning," Earl said at the door. "We talked about you."

Lucia jumped out of bed and widened her eyes. "You don't say. Was it good or bad?"

Earl looked at her and laughed. "You get so excited about Guy it makes one wonder how the doctor will fit into this scenario."

"Shut up," Lucia growled. "Wait, what did you say about me to Guy? Better yet what did he say?"

"Let me see," Earl rubbed his chin, "we discussed the weather, farming, birds—don't ask me how birds came into it, oh and..."

Earl grinned. He exited the room, and Lucia walked after him, tugging down her boy shorts and tying her stretched out t-shirt under her breasts

"Tell me, Earl."

"Nah," Earl said heading for the stove and the hot chocolate her mother had left on the stove.

Aretha was blessedly out of the house and gone for work.

Lucia glanced at the clock. It was a little after seven, which was very late in the valleys, most people started work before dawn.

Lucia had an hour to get ready. She had to reach the supermarket by nine.

Earl looked at her and then at the clock.

"He said he would stop by and drop you to work if you wanted. I told him you might not need the ride because you love taking the bus."

"You did not say that." Lucia groaned. "What's wrong with you? How could you? I don't love taking the staff bus."

Earl laughed. "He will be here by eight."

Lucia made a mad dash back to her room and then looked around the small space as if she were seeing it for the first time.

She had limited options with her wardrobe, the standard blue jeans and green Wiley groceries polo shirts were her uniform, and as a cashier, she was limited in hairstyles too. Her only options were ponytails or slicked back hairstyles. She settled on a deep side part and layered her hair with gel, leaving out two curly tendrils at each side of her ear.

There was no trying to impress Guy, he had seen her a million times in the same old clothes and hairstyles, he wouldn't be bowled over by her this morning, but she could try.

****

Guy showed up at the gate at five minutes to eight. He engaged Earl in conversation about the roof, Lucia surmised because she could see them pointing at it when she attempted to glide out the house a few minutes later.

Guy looked at her and grinned. "Good morning Miss World."

"Hey Guy," Lucia said nonchalantly as if she wasn't struggling to hide the pleased smile face as he looked her over appreciatively.

Her umpteen minutes in front of the mirror had paid off. He called her Miss World!

She pretended to look away while he turned back to Earl but as soon as they started talking about gutters, ripped felts, soffits and roof words she was not familiar with she was looking at him again.

He was simply a beautiful man. There was no other way to describe him. He resembled the picture that the girls were passing around in the break room of the most handsome guy in the world.

The picture was of an Arab man with headgear on. Novalee, her closest friend, had been the one to point out that he looked a lot like Guy. Except that Guy was darker. His eyes more intensely brown and his jet-black hair was lustrous and long. It reached him at his waist. He usually wore it in a fat plait that was enviously thick.

The other girls had expressed disbelief that there was such a man around until he had stopped by one day to buy something and they had all been in shock when they realized that he did exist.

Guy had been unaffected by the attention. He generally was. Guy did not have a drop of vanity in him. It was as if he didn't realize how unique he was.

"Ready?" Guy glanced at his watch and then at her. "I have a thing, and then I am going to buy the roofing materials and then Earl, and I are going to fix this properly."

"Wait, Guy!" Earl said doubtfully, "I'll buy the roofing material."

"Sure," Guy nodded, "when you are financially stable you can pay me back."

Earl nodded. "Yes, I will. Definitely. Thank you."

Guy smiled at him. "See you in a bit then."

Earl nodded again. He could deal with that compromise. He hated charity. They had grown up on it, and he longed to stand on his own.

Guy saw that and accepted it.

Lucia got in the van and sat in the front seat. It was a better-looking one that Guy's usual multicolored rusty van.

"Thank you," Lucia said when Guy started the van.

"For what?" Guy asked glancing at her.

"For helping with the roof. For allowing Earl to contribute to the fix. It's a nice thing to do considering that we are all low on resources."

Guy smiled. "I am not that low on resources. I think I can afford a roof and help you to buy your lens for your first official paying gig."

"Wait!" Lucia groaned, "Earl told you?"

"Yes." Guy slowed down for a herd of goats to cross the road. "Congratulations. I hope you do a fabulous job."

Lucia cleared her throat. "Thank you, but Guy I know you say that you are not low on resources, but this will be too much. The lens is not cheap. It is probably more expensive than the roof, to be honest."

Guy shrugged. "What type of lens is it?"

"I need two lenses' a 24-70 mm and a 70- 200 mm but I will settle for the 24- 70 for now."

"I'll ask my brother Walter if he has that one," Guy said, "he bought a lot of camera equipment two years ago, and he barely uses them."

"Walter Wiley? Vice President of Wiley Corp." Lucia rounded her eyes. "Isn't he one of the rich Wiley's I didn't know you spoke to them."

Guy nodded. "Yes, I speak to them."

"Oh," Lucia nodded, "well if he is willing to lend you his lens I will be more than grateful."

Guy smiled. "I am sure he will lend it to you permanently. He recently got married and has no time for anything else."

"Do you speak to Preston Wiley the head of the business?" Lucia asked interested, Guy never spoke about his brothers or his parents or his past.

She had heard the story of the love triangle between his mother and father and the father's wife from Myrtle. Lucia had assumed that the brothers were not on speaking terms. After all, her own siblings from the Wray side of her family didn't speak to her, and she had been born in a similar situation. The outside child to a married couple.

"Yep, I speak to Preston. The rich Wiley's are not that bad." Guy looked at her and grinned, "Am I more attractive now that I have friends in high places?"

"No," Lucia snorted. "I am not impressed with stuff like that. I was just curious about your family. You know everything about mine, and I know nothing about yours. Well, only what Myrtle told me."

Guy looked at her solemnly. "What did Myrtle tell you?"

Lucia squirmed in her seat. She couldn't tell if he was

angry or not. He looked so serious when he asked.

"She just said your mother was the mistress and your father was married to the supermarket heiress. And that the wife killed them all."

Guy sighed, "That's about right."

"It's not very different from mine except for the killing part," Lucia said sympathetically. "My father and mother were both married when they had an affair and had me. My father's family ignores me even though I look a lot like him."

Guy nodded. "I know. You do look like Mr. Wray, a much prettier version. I saw him at his store yesterday."

"I knew it. You were in Port Antonio. I thought I saw you yesterday too." Lucia frowned.

"Where?" Guy raised an eyebrow at her.

"I went to KFC with Ace." Lucia chuckled dryly. "I was sitting in the restaurant, and I thought I saw you in a nice vehicle, a Range Rover. But it's more than seeing you, I think I felt your presence. It's weird, huh?"

"It's not weird." Guy slowed the vehicle and looked at her curiously. "My mom said she could tell when my father entered a room or a building. In chemistry, some materials move toward each other when they get close to each other. Same with people. It's kind of miraculous, that kind of awareness of another person."

Lucia nodded. "Yes... erm, yes."

She felt embarrassed. He knew she was way more aware of him than she wanted to let on.

"Is that how you feel with Dr. Ace Jackson?" Guy asked casually.

"I don't know." Lucia sighed. "I like him."

She wanted to see Guy's reaction. She half turned to watch him.

He didn't say anything for a while.

The silence almost went on too long. She turned back to the window and was in the middle of watching a yellow tailed bird flicking from tree to tree almost as if it were following them.

They were approaching Bowden Pen square or what they called a square—a smattering of shops and a bus shed was all there was to it. This side of Jamaica was the definition of rural.

Guy finally spoke. "So, you like him?"

He said it so flatly and devoid of emotion that it got Lucia's hackles rising.

"Yes, what's not to like," Lucia said sharply. "He likes me. He thinks I am pretty. I am the reason why he is even in the valleys. He said that he came to close up his father's practice and then move back to Kingston, but instead, he saw me and decided to wait. He sounds serious."

Guy tightened his fist on the steering wheel. "I see."

"That's all you are going to say?" Lucia asked suddenly annoyed with him.

"What do you want me to say?" Guy asked.

"I want you to say..." Lucia paused, she couldn't tell him what she wanted him to say without sounding desperate.

She wanted him to say: *I like you too Lucia, I have liked you for a long time. I am done with playing it safe with you. We have been beating around the bush with each other; it is time we stopped and get serious.*

"There is Novalee." Guy glanced at her while she was in the middle of formulating her thoughts. "You want me to give her a ride?"

"Yes, sure." Lucia subsided in the seat. Nova was always late. She managed to miss the staff bus more often than not.

Lucia glanced at her watch. This morning was an exception. Nova was making an effort.

"I'll pick you up after work so we can continue this conversation," Guy said. "I need to go to the beach side to collect some seaweed this evening."

Lucia nodded eagerly. "Sure."

Guy stopped the vehicle, and Novalee got in, a whiff of flowery perfume followed in her wake.

"Good morning, peoples," Novalee said happily. "I can't believe that I am early enough to get a lift from Guy and to be traveling with my bestie who is never late."

Lucia chuckled. "Never late. It's good to see you out at this time, congrats on the effort."

"Maybe you should get up earlier." Guy smiled at Novalee.

"I never aim to be late." Novalee flicked her blond braids over her shoulder. "It's my family's fault. We have one bathroom and four girls to get ready for work and school. It gets worse when my mother is on the morning shift. That makes five of us. I would do anything to escape the stampede in the morning. I am thinking of moving to Port Antonio. Want to join me, Lucia? I know of a house, the rent is cheap."

Lucia grimaced. "I don't know. Cheap or not, I can't afford it. I want to invest in my photography right now."

Novalee exhaled. "I might need to move from here to keep the job. Since Reggie became a shift manager, he has become vicious. He has threatened to fire me if I'm late one more time."

"Reginald Meeks?" Guy asked, "He got a promotion? Good for him."

"No, not good for him," Novalee hissed. "I can't stand a bone in his bony body."

"He is not that bad," Lucia said gently. "He is just doing his job."

"Oh please," Novalee huffed, "You remember when we were in high school how he used to call us Cream and

Coffee?"

"Yes," Lucia laughed and turned to Guy, "Nova was Cream because she is fair skinned and I was Coffee because I am dark and we were always hanging together."

Guy slowed the vehicle to a crawl to cross the bridge and then looked at Novalee. "That was corny but surely not detestable."

Novalee snorted. "There is something I don't like about him, can't put my finger on it."

"You don't like him because he doesn't like you," Lucia looked back at her friend, "remember he told you that before the entire fourth form class?"

"Yes, that." Novalee growled, "the sicko. He announced it like I had asked him to like me and the whole class thought that I Novalee Rochester would be interested in a slim, anemic looking, spotty faced, wretch like him and now he is my immediate boss. With him around, I will never get employee of the month."

Guy glanced at Lucia. "Employee of the month?"

"For the floor staff." Lucia grimaced. "At the beginning of the month, today actually, we have a mini staff meeting with all the shop floor staff. The general manager, Dominic Black will be there this month."

"The person who is voted employee of the month will be given their incentive. I think it is going to be money this time. The staff is complaining that they don't want anything else."

"Ah," Guy nodded, "I see."

"Dominic...er, Mr. Black will be there?" Nova grinned. "That's nice. He said he liked me, you know."

Lucia frowned. "He said that? Did he mean like as in attracted?"

"Yes," Nova stuck her tongue out at Lucia, "definitely yes.

I can see it in his eyes. If he comes on to me, I am not going to be playing hard to get, oh no. You realize he is the general manager of a supermarket?

"He makes the dollars, baby. He is not a farmer, no offense Guy, but your profession is not a high earning one."

Guy grinned, "No offense taken Novalee but your assumption may be wrong about farmers."

"I doubt that," Novalee snorted, "How many farmers do you know that drives a Mercedes? Dominic drives a Mercedes." Nova turned to Lucia. "You saw the new car?"

"No." Lucia frowned. "I don't like this talk, Novalee. Don't get involved with Dominic just because of his car."

"Oh goodness, no." Nova settled back in her seat. "It's not just the car. He is also building a mansion by the beach in San San, and don't you think he is kind of cute. Not Guy level cute but have you looked at him lately?"

Lucia shook her head. "He looks the same as he always did before the car and the mansion. You should be my mother's daughter. You two would make a lovely pair."

Guy gave her a warm smile after she said that. It was significant. It was a smile of approval. And something else... pride.

She didn't know that what she said would be so pleasing to Guy. She had meant it. She genuinely hated the pursue-the-rich-man mentality. It was super annoying. It was as if nothing else mattered but the fact that they had the outward trappings of wealth. Not their personalities or their compatibility or even their looks.

He could be sloppy and ate children for breakfast but once he was rich, had a nice car or mansion, he was desirable. It was wrong.

"Do you realize I wouldn't be in this predicament if the parish church hadn't transferred my father?" Novalee fumed, "I wouldn't even be living in Bowden Pen if they had administered some kind of Christian mercy and allowed him to stay in his job."

"But didn't he lose thousands of dollars of the church's money?" Lucia asked doubtfully.

"Lose is right. I am happy you didn't say steal." Novalee sighed, "we didn't see a dime of that money. The bishop took the money without permission to help out a few of his parishioners at his discretion. To transfer him to Bowden Pen in the stinking valleys in a two-bedroom hidey-hole is his punishment. It's like jail. That two-bedroom manse, if you can call it that, is a rat haven."

"Get a cat." Lucia smiled.

"No thanks, hate the nasty furry creatures almost as much as the rats."

"Have you no soul?" Lucia gasped. "Cats are the best animals on the planet, and they are not nasty. Dogs are also good with rats."

"Hate them too." Novalee grinned and then changed the topic. "I wonder what it would be like to drive in a Mercedes."

As if on cue Guy's vehicle backfired loudly when they reached the town.

Novalee shouted in laughter. "Absolutely not like this."

Guy and Lucia laughed with her.

"Pick you up at three," Guy said when he dropped them at the supermarket.

The van took a while to start. Lucia watched as Guy finally got it going. He looked at her and grinned, not an ounce of shame in his face or apology for the attention he was getting from the malfunctioning vehicle.

He waved at her when it finally moved, and Lucia waved back.

Lucia couldn't wait for their evening outing. She didn't

mind driving in an old vehicle once she was driving with Guy.

Her mother would call her unambitious, but she didn't care.

Chapter Five

The mini staff meeting was held in the conference room upstairs.

Reggie dramatically widened his eyes when he saw Nova walking in behind Lucia. He gave them a lopsided grin and a thumbs up. His behavior was unlike the monster that Nova was trying to paint him to be.

Lucia grinned back. Nova narrowed her eyes at him and snarled.

Reggie grinned even wider.

The meeting got off to a prompt start. Dominic Black gave them an inspirational talk about being kind. It was a talk worthy of an amen, which the staff gave him with gusto.

Novalee was sighing beside her and making cow eyes at him. Lucia forced herself not to pinch Nova so would stop her nonsense, especially when Dominic looked over at their side of the room and Nova slowly opened three buttons of her shirt.

"He is so fine, like Mahershela Ali, that actor guy with the perfect smile."

"Mahershela Mercedes Benz." Lucia snickered.

Novalee stopped her fawning long enough to glare at Lucia. "I have no idea why we are still friends. You just don't get it."

"Me neither," Lucia muttered. "Because I think you are the one who doesn't get it."

The employee of the month award went to Acadia Reid. She got a plaque with her picture. It would be placed near the cashiers' stations for all to see and best of all she got a substantial check. She was clearly excited.

The management had accomplished what they had intended with the gift. Everybody was determined to be the next employee of the month.

After the meeting, even Novalee was vowing to wake up from three o'clock to get ready for work.

Lucia planned to smile more at the customers and be more pleasant in general. That was what Acadia had over the lot of them; the girl was just nice and helpful. She was kind as Dominic had said.

It shone out of her; it was as if she was born with customer service in her blood. Of the eight cashiers in the busy supermarket she was the most popular with customers and with good reason—customers were allowed to vote.

"Maybe the rest of us will stand a chance at employee of the month when little miss sunshine is no longer sleeping with Reggie," Novalee said snarkily.

It was lunchtime. They were sitting together in the break room in their usual spot. It was in the far corner overlooking the parking lot and the sea on the opposite side of the road.

"Keep your voice down." Lucia hissed after Novalee's uncharitable outburst.

"She is though," Novalee snorted, "and I am not hating. I am just stating a fact. Since she hooked up with Reggie, she has been employee of the month three months in a row."

"How do you know they are seeing each other?" Lucia whispered. Unlike Nova, she was not going to be spewing absolutes about people without proof.

"Because Lila from accounts saw them one night in Reggie's car at the Marina. They were not just holding hands."

"Oh," Lucia widened her eyes.

"And here comes the devil," Novalee said under her breath when Reggie strode into the lunchroom, with his meal from Yum Yum Cafe on a tray with his mini television. He looked over at them and smiled.

"I see you are making an effort to be early, Novalee. Who knows, maybe one day you will be employee of the month."

Novalee smirked. "I don't have what it takes to be the employee of the month if it involves long date nights in the dark, in your car, at the Marina."

Reggie frowned. "So you listen to gossip, it is not surprising. Just don't repeat it. Acadia is a lovely woman, and she deserved her award. No extracurricular activities involved."

"As for you Lucia, you are in the running for the employee of the month, next month. Just be careful of the company you keep."

Lucia sighed. "Why can't you and Novalee just get along?"

"I have several professional reasons why I have issues with Novalee Rochester and personal issues too which only she and I know about." Reggie sat down, plunked his headphones in his ears and proceeded to watch a Youtube video.

"Personal reasons?" Lucia raised an eyebrow at Nova. "What is that about?"

"It's nothing." Novalee made a face and looked down at her empty plate. "He is stuck in high school mode. I sort of had a little thing with him."

"With Reggie?" Lucia widened her eyes. "How comes I didn't know that?"

"It was three years ago when I repeated fifth form. He rejected me in fourth form; I had to prove that he was petty, so I pursued him. We are all adults now. I don't know why he is even bringing it up."

"You know what, I need another job," Novalee murmured looking down at her empty plate. "Something along the lines of lady of leisure."

Lucia chuckled. "It was a regular conversational topic for Nova."

"I am so serious." Nova cupped her hand under her chin. "Why am I not a lady of leisure? I have the looks; I constantly hear that I am a dead ringer for Beyonce. And I did come third in the parish beauty pageant."

Lucia shook her head. "Don't start this again."

This was Novalee's regular mantra since they both started work at Wiley Groceries almost at the same time.

Novalee was a pretty girl. She had a warm golden skin tone, hazel eyes, long brown hair that she currently had dyed in blond.

"But why not?" Nova moaned, "I am working as a cashier at a supermarket. I should be wined and dined and fawned over by some rich dude, like say Dominic Black."

"So we are back to that." Lucia raised an eyebrow. "You better be careful with men like Dominic. He doesn't strike me as someone who likes to play games. Besides, isn't he engaged or something?"

"Or something. Who knows?" Nova grinned at her cheekily, "If it's not Dominic, it has to be the next eligible bachelor in

Portland, Ace Jackson. I took my little sister, Jilly, to him last week and he is so fine. The best looking doctor we've had in this sleepy old town in years. Now I know why your mother is insisting that you take notice."

"I think he likes me," Novalee said contemplatively, "when he was filling out Jilly's prescription he winked at me and gave me his business card."

Lucia chuckled. "He gives everybody his business card."

"I think I am special. He took one look at me, and he could envision me by his side. I would make the perfect doctor's wife."

Novalee ran her finger along the edge of her glass slowly and said dreamily. "Now, who do I choose? The gorgeous doctor or the general manager of the supermarket where I work?

"Both of them are single, both of them are wealthy. Only one of them drives a new Mercedes, though."

Lucia snickered.

"Don't get me wrong, those two are great options," Novalee looked at Lucia sternly, "but Guy Wiley is amazing to look at. I can't quite get Guy out of my mind."

Lucia sat up straighter and scowled. "Leave Guy out of your little manhunt."

Novalee cackled. "If I wanted Guy you would not stand a chance. The reason he is not in contention boils down to three things."

Novalee started counting on her fingers. "One, he is a farmer, two, he is not one of the moneyed Wiley's and three, he drives that battered van. Otherwise, he would be at the very top of my list, and you couldn't do a thing about it. We would make the most amazing babies together, Guy and I. Can you imagine that?"

Lucia got up. "No, and I don't ever want to."

"Oh stop being jealous." Nova got up too. "I am in an upwardly mobile frame of mind. As pretty as your precious Guy is, I will have to give him a pass. If you had any sense, you would do the same. Unless of course, your future plans are to rot in Bowden Pen with the rest of the no-hope-of-escape crew."

"Don't go off judging me, Lucia." Nova followed her out of the cafeteria. "You can afford to be picky about your men and have romantic thoughts about men like Guy. You have no clue about what it is like to grow up rough like I did."

"What?" Lucia stopped and spun around. "Where is this madness coming from?"

"We didn't all grow up with charity society's catering to our every need," Nova said peevishly. "They built your family a house and buy your groceries and clothes and expensive shoes. They spoilt you."

"Because we were at the lowest of the low," Lucia said heatedly. "If you are poor then I was poorer than poor. We lived in the Alms House! You have a mother and father and both of them work!

"They have good jobs. Your father is a bishop, and your mother is a teacher. They are both college educated, and you don't pay rent."

"But the seven of us live in a tiny house," Novalee said, "just two rooms and one bathroom. You have your own room and bathroom, thanks to the Farm Help Society."

"Lord give me strength," Lucia rolled her eyes. "Do you know what it is like to go to bed hungry? To not have a roof over your head? To brush your teeth with salt because you can't afford toothpaste, to walk around in homemade cardboard bottom shoes because you don't have proper shoes?

"To wear your mother's old threadbare curtains that she

made into dresses because you don't have any clothes?"

Novalee shrugged. "Well no, but you do realize that the Farm Help Society only helps your family, don't you? And since then you have gotten only the best clothes and shoes and things."

"And God bless them, you should only give your best to people even if they are destitute. I am not arguing with you about this, and at work at that," Lucia hissed. She was feeling very disappointed in Novalee.

Obviously, her so-called friend was jealous of her getting charity. Who did that? Who was jealous of the poor receiving charity?"

She had no idea that Nova thought that way.

"You should ask yourself who they are?" Novalee shouted loudly in the hallway. "Who are these Farm Help Society people who have made it so that you Lucia Wray can walk around as if you are better than the rest of us!"

Chapter Six

Lucia repeated the conversation to Guy as soon as she got in the van. At least the part about the Farm Help Society. She was still fuming at Novalee.

She didn't act as if she was better than anyone. How could she act that way?

"I lived in the poor house!" Lucia exclaimed for the third time. "She has her mother and father who have done nothing but support her and she thinks I act better than her. Ridiculous! If the Bishop only knew what a mean petty, self-centered, narcissistic, jealous..."

Guy listened to her patiently.

They drove along the sea wall while she fumed. They passed Trident in the distance and then headed toward the Drapers area. She hardly came to this end of Portland even though she lived in the parish. In fact, she hadn't been anywhere outside of Portland. This was all she knew.

She was a total country bumpkin. What on earth had given

her the idea that she could go to Kingston to shoot a wedding?

Everybody would take one look at her and know that she was an amateur. Then she realized that she had gone silent after talking nonstop about Nova and was thinking about the wedding gig.

Her first paying job.

She glanced at Guy sheepishly. "Sorry about the vent, I had that backed up in me all day. I may have growled at a customer or two. I can forget about the employee of the month next month. Nobody from today would vote for me."

"It's okay." Guy smiled. "I think you deserve to vent now and again."

"How was your day?" Lucia asked belatedly.

"We took off the roofing material, found the cause of the problem and replaced it."

"All in a days work, huh?" Lucia grinned at him. "Thank you."

It was not a problem. Guy shrugged, "I would do anything for you."

Lucia's heart lurched. "Do you mean that in a family friend kind of way or a Guy likes Lucia kind of way?"

Guy turned to her and smiled. "What do you think?"

"I've known you for five years, and I still have to ask." Lucia frowned, "Do you have a girlfriend?"

"No." Guy raised an eyebrow at her. "If I had a girlfriend then you'd probably know by now. I spend a good chunk of my time around you. We talk quite a bit, you and I. Surely a girlfriend would come up in one of our conversations."

"I know that but..." Lucia sighed. "You don't like Novalee do you?"

"What a question?" Guy chuckled, "I don't dislike her."

"She said that if she wanted you, I would not stand a chance."

Guy laughed. "Do you want a chance?"

Lucia avoided answering. "I just told her to take you out of her manhunt talk."

"I like that you are looking out for me," Guy stopped the van near a hut that had a big sign that read Brushy's, Seaweeds For Sale. "But surely you must know that Novalee thinks I am too poor to waste her time on me."

"Yes," Lucia nodded, "she is thinking of escaping Bowden Pen at all cost."

Guy turned to Lucia. "Isn't that what you want to do too? You told me you hated rural living."

"I do want to spread my wings. There is no harm in that." Lucia sighed, "I want to travel, see the world. Do you realize that when I go to Kingston, it will be my first time leaving Portland?"

"Yes," Guy nodded, "I understand perfectly. Where will you stay?"

"I have no idea." Lucia sighed. "I just know that the wedding will be at a fancy place in Kingston."

Guy winked. "Don't worry about it. I'll ask my brother to find you somewhere to stay. They live in a townhouse complex. There is always a house available there."

"I don't want to impose." Lucia widened her eyes. When she pictured the rich Wiley's, she imagined them being cold and unfriendly. Why else would they have their brother being a poor farmer and not help him?

"Oh, it won't be a problem." Guy grinned. "They owe me."

Lucia nodded doubtfully. "I guess so."

Brushy came to the door of his shack and peered out at them. He was shirtless, his beard almost hitting him in the chest and his dreadlocks hitting him at his knee.

"Guy Wiley! Respect man. I've got more seaweed than you can handle."

"Never." Guy grinned. "I can't get enough."

Lucia watched as he piled large bags of seaweed into the back of the van. She got out to offer to help, but Guy and Brushy turned her down.

Brushy whistled at her. "My goodness, what a pretty lady! Is this your queen, Guy?"

Guy paused for a second and looked at her meaningfully. "I want her to be, but I am just a humble farmer, these pretty girls don't make for very good farmers wives. They want to escape the quiet farming life for the bright city lights."

Brushy laughed. "I know what you mean. There is a reason why the term homely was used to describe some women. They were the ones most likely to stay home, and this potential queen could hold her own on a runway in Paris. Maybe you should get a homely girl and leave me with this one. I don't mind the city lights."

"This one's name is Lucia," Lucia scowled.

"And feisty," Brushy murmured good-naturedly. "She makes me miss Mabel."

Guy hefted the last bag of seaweed in the van. "Where is Mabel?"

"Left me to go back to her people in the hills. Your hills up in St. Andrew near the strawberry farm." Brushy sighed. "I have to go and get her back for the fiftieth time. I also have to think about quitting tobacco seriously. She hates when I chew it. She calls it a disgusting habit."

Guy chuckled. "Good luck."

Lucia watched as Guy paid Brushy and then bid him a friendly goodbye.

"Why do you need the seaweeds anyway?" Lucia asked as they drove off. "And why are you so happy to be a farmer? I never understood that. You do know that you would fair better on a runway in Paris than me."

Guy glanced at her. "You calling me pretty again?"

"No," Lucia giggled. "I am not calling you that, I am just thinking it."

Guy shook his head. "Cheeky."

"I am serious, Guy." Lucia looked at him puzzled. "You are so good-looking, and you went to college, and you are young. Why did you take this path in life?"

"Because I love it." Guy shrugged. "I've always known I would be a farmer. I've always known I would work with the soil. I've always wanted to live a quiet life. To help you understand me a bit more, I am going to show you my childhood home and my first garden."

Lucia nodded eagerly. "Cool. A glimpse into your mysterious past."

"My earlier years with my mom was good. She was a hairdresser; my dad ran the supermarket where you now work. I lived with my older brother Jordan, and then my baby brother came along, and everything was good. I had no idea that my father had another family, a wife and three other boys. You don't know these things at age nine or even care to know. My dad spent most of his time with us anyway. It was not as if he was an absentee father."

Lucia nodded. "He did?"

"Yes," Guy nodded, "and then one day after school, the pastor's wife met me at the gate and told me I couldn't go home. I will have to stay with them for the next couple of days because both my mother and father were dead and my home was a crime scene. I didn't understand, couldn't process it at first.

"She took me to her home, and I saw my brother Jordan on the veranda crying his heart out. He grabbed me and hugged me, and I started crying too."

"Oh goodness," Lucia murmured. "That's just so sad."

Guy stopped at a house at the corner of Spring Street.

"This it is, where I grew up." He got out of the van and opened the van from her side.

"I am going to show you the reason why I am a farmer."

Lucia got out eagerly. "Does anybody live here?"

"No." Guy opened the gate, and she walked behind him, he went to the side of the house and to a well-kept backyard. At the back were some raised beds with green, healthy looking plants.

"My dad and I," Guy said proudly, "this is where we hung out every weekend. We had this routine, something that he practiced with only me. I don't know why, but it certainly shaped the way I saw life and farming.

"I don't know how old I was, maybe he was doing it from I was a baby, but every Saturday and Sunday morning, very early when everybody was still in bed, we would sit under that mahogany tree after we did whatever we needed to do for the plants... He would allow me to water or weed them."

Guy pointed to the mahogany tree where some stone benches were. "Come on let's go."

Lucia walked behind him looking around. Everything was so lush.

"My dad would start out by saying, farmers work too much and work too hard. They should be farming by faith and not by works."

Guy chuckled. "He wasn't a churchman, but he sure knew how to bring some points across."

Lucia sat beside him. "What did he mean by farming by faith?"

Guy pointed to the raised beds. "Most farmers who farm by works they dig up the ground, they weed, or spray the weeds and insects, they do a lot of work to prepare the soil as they like to put it but the farmer who farms by faith recognizes that God has set up a system that is designed to be self-sufficient."

"So the one who farms by faith studies nature and decides to mimic the things they see in nature."

"In the natural system, one thing you don't see is the uncovered soil. So a faith-based farmer will cover the soil with organic matter, which will provide a habitat for beneficial insects as well as nutrients for the plants. In turn, the plant will be more healthy and more pest resistant.

"Instead of chemical-based fertilizers, I apply seaweed which provides micronutrients to the plants. The seaweeds collect nutrients from the sea floor, so when it washes ashore, it still contains these nutrients. For plants to reach their full genetic potential, you have to recreate Edenic conditions for them."

Lucia nodded. "Oh, I see!"

"My dad and I would get seaweed from the beach and feed the soil; we were rewarded with the biggest and juiciest vegetables because the plants got what they needed naturally."

"Oh, wow." Lucia nodded. "I get it now. While farming you feel close to your dad."

"Yes," Guy nodded, "there is that, and there is the fact that I just love it. I feel closest to God on a farm than at a church. Not to mention the fact that plants teach you all sorts of lessons."

"Like what?" Lucia leaned back and looked up in the glossy mahogany leaves.

"Like relationship lessons," Guy leaned back with her, bracing his hands on the stone table, "I am a strawberry farmer."

"And the strawberries are delicious," Lucia chuckled. "I wish you would invite me to the farm where you work. I have never seen a strawberry plant."

Guy nodded. "Okay, I will invite you, one day."

"I get two weeks off in June…after my wedding gig," Lucia said. "Just to let you know when."

Guy smiled. "I hear you. It is also the very best time on the farm. My brother got married up there last year."

"He did? Which one?"

"Walter." Guy smiled. "He knows the owner. It was a lovely wedding."

"Tell me what you learned from strawberries," Lucia said. "You were going to tell me a lesson."

"Strawberries are sweet and fragrant and so delicate, they are a member of the rose family you know? Which includes the very lovely smelling plants that we call roses."

"For real?" Lucia murmured. "I learn something new from you every day."

"Anyway," Guy ran a finger gently across her jawline. "The strawberry plant can be finicky and pretty demanding, the temperature, the soil, the water, the sun or shade has to be just right, or else you may not get the best tasting or looking strawberries. If you get any fruits at all. Strawberries take a lot of work.

"On the other hand, there are a few mango trees on the farm. Five years ago, I got a few seedlings, of the Keitt variety. You know that variety, right?"

"Yes!" Lucia nodded vigorously. "Oh, I love Keitt mangos, my favorite mango."

"Well, I have a couple of them." Guy smiled, "I planted them, made sure that I penned them around. So that animals or humans wouldn't trouble them.

"Initially, I watered them and mulched them to give them the best chance at survival. I left them alone after that. They didn't need me to be there for them like the strawberries. I allowed them to do their thing."

"This year I have hundreds of green fruit on the trees. It's amazing. I have to tell you, I love my strawberries, but they are not necessarily ride or die plants. The least provocation and they won't bear fruit."

Lucia stared at Guy transfixed. He was so passionate about farming that his entire face was transformed when he spoke about it. It was as if it glowed from an inner light.

He looked at her solemnly. "You can compare it to relationships, strawberries are sweet and with the right conditions will give you some lovely fruits, but they are high maintenance, mangoes, on the other hand, grow into independent trees, they weather storms, bear fruit without much assistance and are far more resilient and longer lasting. That's what I want, a mango tree type of a relationship."

Lucia nodded. "A mango tree type of a relationship. Cool, I get that."

"And now let me give you a tour of the inside," Guy said grinning. "I hope I didn't bore you with my farm talk."

"No." Lucia got up and looked at him contemplatively, "no, you didn't."

Chapter Seven

"**I** am sure that I bored her with my talk of mangos and strawberries." Guy paced Walter's back patio.

Walter grinned. "I am sure you didn't."

"The doctor would never have said something so fruity." Guy tugged at his earlobe and then stopped.

His brothers were staring at him with various expressions of amusement. It was rare for all of them to be around at the same time these days. He spent the majority of his time in the hills between Portland and his farm in St. Andrew.

Case spent the majority of his time touring.

Jordan was working on a huge Wiley hotel project in Montego Bay. He had all but moved there with Shawn and their daughter Courtney.

Walter was still floating around in honeymoon land, and Preston was overseeing a new project in Cayman.

When Walter found out that they would all be around for the weekend, he had thrown a brother's only party. It featured root beer that Micky had brewed himself. Micky had given Guy cases of it when he last visited.

Guy took a sip of the dark liquid and nodded. It wasn't bad. It was a bit heavy on the roots and slightly bitter, but Micky had claimed it was a cure-all. According to Micky, it had cured him of alcoholism. He had been sober since his first brew. So there had to be some truth to it. He hadn't seen Micky sober in years.

Guy took another sip and raised an eyebrow at Saint. His brother looked downcast and pensive, unusually so.

"What happened to Sandrene? I didn't see her when I stopped by Preston's house to deliver the root beer. Aisha, Shawn, and Sheryl were having a party of their own, but there was no Sandrene."

"Don't change the subject." Saint took a sip of his beer. "Go on with your experiment story."

"Yes," Walter nodded quickly, "on with the story."

Guy frowned something wasn't right. He needed to have a one on one with Saint and maybe Walter. Something was going on.

"That's the story," he said sitting down across from his brothers. "Oh Walter, I need your camera lenses, you don't use them anyway."

"I was going to use them someday," Walter grumbled, "but your businesses keep expanding and creating more work for little old me. I have no time for new hobbies."

"Can Lucia have it?" Guy asked impatiently.

"Yes," Walter said grudgingly. "She can have it."

"And you are going to invite her to stay in my townhouse when she comes to Kingston. Pretend it's just a guest house at the complex."

"Sure." Walter nodded. "It is a guest house; you are never here."

"And no one is to tell her that I am not exactly destitute."
Guy looked at them meaningfully.

"This is ridiculous," Preston murmured. "You know that
right? Just tell her that you are loaded, you are the ridiculous
charity organization that has been financing her family for
the past five years and let the chips fall where they may."

"No, wait!" Jordan frowned, "I understand his plan. He
wants her to choose him for himself, warts and all. I can get
behind that."

"I don't like it." Case pointed his beer bottle at Guy. "You
sir are playing with fire. If you love her, why risk losing her.
It's like you planting one of your crops and letting someone
else reap it. Can you stand by while this Doctor Ace marries
your woman? A woman he wouldn't have looked at twice if
you hadn't been tending, watering and supporting her?"

"I am with you on this one, Guy." Saint steepled his fingers
under his chin. "I think if you reveal who you are to her
like Preston says, you'll never know what she feels for you
because I can guarantee that she'll be obligated to be with
you after she finds out. Even if there was no doctor in the
picture, you have a right to feel loved for yourself and not
for your money."

"But she seems to like him already," Preston said. "What's
the use carrying on the charade?"

"Maybe because I am cognizant of the fact that she needs
to explore, step out of the bubble she has been living in
and spread her wings." Guy sighed, "I may be ready for a
relationship, but I doubt she is. You know, last week she said
she has never left Portland in her entire life. Lucia needs
some exposure."

"Then take her on a world tour." Preston grinned. "Let
Walter plan it for you."

"That's a lovely idea," Walter nodded, "but I'd advise

you to start small. Take her on a tour of Jamaica first and then take a month of the year every year and visit the world alphabetically. Start with Australia, Britain, Canada, Dominica, Egypt, etc."

Guy chuckled. "Sounds like something you would like to do."

"Oh, yes." Walter nodded, "Aisha and I have discussed doing something like that before we have children. Maybe you and Lucia could come along. I'll let you know."

Guy grimaced. "I don't know about that. I am quite happy in my corner of the world. I have no longing to explore."

"You are going to have to compromise and move out of farmer mode now and again." Jordan murmured, "you can leave the plants for a while and explore new places, a few times per year, instead of expecting her to be in the countryside like you do. If you plop her down in one place when she wants adventure, she will get bored. Nobody will love farming like you. I mean it, nobody. You have to consider that."

The rest of the brother's chuckled.

"That way," Jordan continued, "you get the best of both worlds, your farming life, and a happy wife."

Guy rested back in the chair and nodded. "Okay. I hear you. I could rouse myself to go other places. Good advice, Jordan."

"And he is the best person to give wife advice," Saint murmured. "Shawn she seems extremely happy these days."

Jordan chuckled. "I can't take credit, Shawn loves working on big projects. This one in Mobay is pretty challenging. She loves challenges, thrives on them. Walks around with a big grin when we solve something and we come in under budget."

"So what about you?" Guy asked Saint. "Why can't you

give advice and why is Sandrene missing?"

"Because she is crazy, that's why," Saint said heatedly. "She has changed beyond recognition. I don't know if I am going to last the year with her."

"Woah," Guy widened his eyes, "say what?"

Walter sighed and turned to Saint. "I thought you were going to give this some serious consideration before saying anything."

Saint shook his head. "I can't hide it anymore. My wife and I are on the verge of a split. And when she goes, I say, good riddance."

Everybody but Walter seemed surprised.

Guy frowned. "Why?"

"First she had Gracie staying with us for three solid months while she got her apartment redone," Saint snarled. "I detest Gracie."

"The twin sister with the big butt and the reams of fake hair such that you can't see her face?" Guy grimaced.

"Ugh," Preston and Jordan snorted at the same time.

There was no love for Gracie among the Wiley brothers. She somehow managed to scream overdone and fake and with an attitude to match.

Saint ran his fingers through his curly brown hair. "Gracie removed the fake butt and hair and over the top stuff and went back to her normal self. She stayed with us for a while and the next thing I know she is twinning hard with Sandrene.

"She had Sandrene starving herself down to a size zero and going to the gym. And then next thing I know they are wearing their hair the same and talking the same and giggling the same."

"I am afraid my wife was made over into her sister's image, not just looks, but personality too. I didn't marry Gracie. I married Sandrene. My sweet, lovely wife who was warm and kind and didn't have a superficial bone in her body is now much like her sister.

"One day I got in from work, they were both sitting at the breakfast nook, and I couldn't tell who was Sandrene and who was Gracie! I know they were identical, but I could always tell who is who but that night I honestly couldn't tell who was my wife and who was Gracie."

"Oh, my," Guy muttered, silence reigned for a full minute.

"Ask Gracie to leave immediately," Jordan said afterward.

"I didn't need to." Saint snorted. "She left a couple of weeks ago to go to Grenada to be with her new boyfriend who wants her there on a trial basis or something."

"At first, I was like good riddance, but the problem here is that I feel as if Gracie never left. I am living with Gracie number two, my old wife the one I fell in love with is gone.

"And this new Sandrene is hounding me for children and a renewal of our vows and all sorts of nonsense when the truth is, I don't have it anymore. The attraction is gone. I lost it. I feel nothing for my wife. It has been a month, and there are no improvements.

"Have you thought of counseling?" Preston asked, "It could help."

"No, it won't help." Saint sighed. "She threatened to move back to her parents' place. They are not here, though. They are in Australia helping their son start up his new restaurant, and Gracie is not here, so Sandrene is managing their restaurant here. She said she has to leave because of my attitude. I offered to help her pack."

Guy gasped. "But Saint you loved her so much."

"And I lost it." Saint frowned in puzzlement, "it's gone. I honestly thought I'd love her forever, but the love has disappeared."

"Love doesn't disappear like that," Preston murmured.

"Make an effort to make it work."

"I don't know if I want to." Saint took a big gulp of his beer, "I just don't want to."

"And here I thought that I had a problem," Guy muttered. "I honestly thought you two were the real deal."

"I guess we are the strawberries in that little analogy you gave to Lucia," Saint muttered. "We definitely don't have a mango tree type of a relationship."

****

"Lucia likes Guy Wiley," Aretha said to Ace as soon as he stepped through the front door. The old door looked shiny like it was recently waxed.

When his housekeeper was in cleaning mode, she did so with vigor. They ran through bottles of furniture polish every week. The old house had never been so clean.

"That's a depressing greeting, Aretha." Ace grimaced. "It wasn't a particularly cheerful day at work, there is a stomach bug going around and now this."

"They went shopping for seaweed yesterday, and he gave her some speech about being a strawberry or a mango tree. And she came home determined to be a mango tree."

Ace frowned. "Huh?"

"You are literally losing in this," Aretha muttered. "Like completely lost. I don't know what else I can do. I can't lock her up in the house and forbid her to see him. She's too old for that."

Aretha gave him a stern frown. "Why are you moving so slow? It has been a year! The more you do your little refined courting or whatever it is you are doing, she is slipping through your fingers!"

Ace closed the door and leaned on it. He could see his

reflection in the hardwood floor beneath his feet, and he was struggling to keep up with his housekeeper who was looking at him as fiercely as if she would deck him over the head with her handbag.

"I have never had to court anybody before. It's a bit old fashioned don't you think? Besides, your daughter is reserved. Very reserved."

"You can't expect that she'll like you just because you are a doctor." Aretha crossed her hands over her chest and frowned. "My Lucia is not one of those girls who'll be frightened by your profession. I don't understand why. We were almshouse poor and practically living in the streets, and this girl has no appreciation for the finer things in life."

Ace nodded. "I remember the story. A charity rescued you."

"Yes, the Farm Help Society." Aretha nodded. "Thank the father, the son and the Holy Spirit for the charity, but I am afraid that if Lucia continues with this farmer Guy Wiley, she will be going back to charity. You have to rescue her, Dr. Jackson. She is young and foolish."

"Rescue her?" Ace frowned, "are they involved?"

"Not yet." Aretha shook her head, "Guy is slow like you, but I should tell you that your workmen didn't fix that roof properly, Guy and my son Earl had to fix it. If this were a competition, I'd say Guy one, and you zero."

"Wait a minute!" Ace frowned. "I had no idea the roof was still leaking."

"It was." Aretha nodded. "But now it isn't. And as bad as I would want to tell Guy to leave my house. He just fixed my roof."

"I have to go," Aretha said glancing at her watch, "my big son is here. I did beef lasagna. It is still in the oven and piping hot. I also got an invitation from a Mrs. Hightower;

it's on there."

Aretha pointed to a white envelope on the entryway table.

Ace nodded. "It's the annual chamber of commerce ball and awards ceremony."

"Maybe you could take Lucia. Show her off. Give her a taste of that kind of thing. That's something that could one-up Guy Wiley. I doubt if he has ever worn anything formal in his life."

Chapter Eight

Ace sat on his back patio after Aretha left. It was late evening and quiet. Too quiet. The birds that were a constant source of background noise were silent. The air was still, and the sky was starless. It was going to rain.

He looked over at his leafy kingdom and felt the first chords of boredom reaching into his chest and tightening its fist slowly and ever so tightly. He was tired of living alone. It was that palpable and that profound. He wanted companionship. No, not want it was a need. He was too young to be living like an old retiree in the middle of nowhere, in his parent's old manor house. He missed the city and his friends.

And he wanted Lucia to be by his side.

He was too in love with her. He had never felt this way before, and it scared him.

Sometimes, the wicked thought came to him that he should use any means necessary to get her to relax around him to stop her being so skittish, but he banished the thought. He wanted to do things the right way with Lucia. He wanted her to love him.

He wanted the kind of relationship his parents had. He could remember his father saying that there was nothing his mother could do that would make him leave her.

Ace wanted that kind of commitment.

And yet sometimes he thought, maybe Lucia was not worth hanging around for. Maybe he didn't want to be in a competition for her hand with Guy Wiley. The nasty thought cropped up in his head, and he quickly squelched it.

She was worth it.

He got up and stretched. When he felt this way, he usually needed to take a walk, stretch his legs and brush out the old cobwebs.

He grabbed his raincoat, flashlight, water boots, and cell phone. Ironically, he loved to walk when it rained. He didn't mind the lack of clarity or the wet, cold feeling when the water hit his raincoat. It made him feel enervated. He took the winding driveway all the way to the gate.

Micky Wiley, his very unreliable gardener who only showed up when he felt like it had flanked the driveway with fragrant plants. He could smell the lavender in the semi-dark. He grudgingly admitted that it was a pleasant addition to the landscape. Micky did things in his own time and at his leisure, but over the past year, he had completely transformed the acreage into a respectable garden.

At age seventy, he moved faster, than many men half his age and was more meticulous and caring about the plants than even his mother who had been an avid gardener when she lived there.

Ace found himself walking in the direction of Micky's hill. He lived about half a mile from the manor. Micky had a persistent cold but refused to take modern medicine for it.

Ace had not seen him for a whole week and a half; he needed to check on him. He had a soft spot for Micky. Maybe he could ferret out some information about Guy Wiley. He was Micky's nephew, and they were pretty close.

As he knew it would, the path was dark, and the rain came down in torrents. He turned his face up to the silver drops and laughed in glee. He had a playful side that very few persons saw. He reveled in things like this. The walk was beneficial as he knew it would be. When he took the asphalted road all the way to the top of the steep incline to Micky's place, he was grateful for two things: Micky's family had put in an asphalt road and that he had brought the flashlight.

Ace was surprised to see that there was a bright enough light on the veranda. Myrtle Wiley was sitting in a rocking chair humming and crocheting, her fingers flying over the needles rapidly, a pretty crocheted design pooled in her lap.

"Hello Myrtle," Ace called before advancing toward the veranda. He didn't want to startle her.

Myrtle looked up at him and smiled, her fingers not missing a beat, still doing a weird dance with the needle and thread.

Myrtle was his parents' housekeeper, and he had wanted her to continue, but she had suggested that he use Aretha Gordon instead.

That's how he had met Lucia.

He still remembered seeing Lucia for the first time. It had been as if time had stood still.

She was in a white summer dress with some tiny flowers all over it. The sun had hit her eyes just when she had looked at him. They had been a gorgeous deep brown shade.

The thought of her put a smile on his face. He had marveled that such a lovely girl lived in the countryside.

"Doctor Ace!" Myrtle beamed at him. "Come in out of the rain."

He did just that, removing his heavy dripping raincoat and hanging it on a hook beside the door.

"I just thought I would take a walk." He swiped the water from his brows. "I haven't seen Micky in a while. Thought I would check on him."

"He is fine." Myrtle smirked, "better than fine. He has taken up beer making. Not the alcoholic kind," she quickly added.

"He is heeding what you said about the alcohol. He wanted to cure his cold and then developed this formula that tasted like the root beer we used to drink as children. Guy brought him bottles and set up a sterilized area for him, and he has been boiling and cooling and tweaking the formula and driving me crazy with tasting it.

"Stay right there," Myrtle got up and went into the house. She returned shortly after with a dark beer bottle and handed it to him. "Taste this."

Ace looked at it doubtfully and then cleared his throat. "Now Myrtle, I am not herbally inclined."

Myrtle laughed. "Herbally inclined? I like that. This one is so good I think it solved the arthritic pain I had in my fingers."

"Really?" Ace took the bottle.

Myrtle handed him a can opener that was lying on a wicker table close where she was sitting and watched him keenly as he opened the bottle, sniffed it and then tentatively took a sip.

He widened his eyes.

"What's in this?"

"Hops, licorice, birch, juniper, sarsaparilla, sassafras, and ginger." Myrtle grinned at him. "The licorice makes it sweet, and the ginger gives it a kick."

"I'd say," Ace took another sip. "It's not bad."

"That's what Guy said," Myrtle chuckled. "I told him that Micky has his use."

"He does." Ace nodded. "Where is he by the way?"

"Went down to George's shop to play dominoes." Myrtle sighed. "I told him it would rain and he didn't even take his raincoat."

"Stubborn man," Ace murmured.

"It's in the Wiley genes." Myrtle chuckled. "All the men are stubborn. Some more than others but all of them have that streak."

Ace sat back in the chair and crossed his ankles. "Tell me about Guy Wiley. I don't know anything much about him except that he drives that eyesore that you can hear from a mile away and he's a farmer and Lucia seems to think the sun rises and sets on him.

"All the girls think so," Myrtle took up her crochet piece and whistled. "He is a very handsome man."

"But does he think that way about her?" Ace murmured lazily, but he was on high alert waiting for Myrtle's answer. He had been discomfited ever since his conversation with Aretha.

"I can't say yes, and I can't say no," Myrtle said vaguely. "Guy doesn't talk much. He is an action kind of man. Whenever he comes here, he helps out Micky with one project after another.

"See, we now have electricity. Guy put in a couple of them solar things for us and a wind turbine. Next time he said he is going to put in lights all around the property and I am finally going to get a television, to keep me company in the nights when Micky is gone to George's shop."

Ace nodded. "So, he is a good nephew?"

"The best, I think." Myrtle nodded, "the very best. I tell you not many men his age have the time for the older set.

He is kind to a fault. And he is patient. He has slowly and cleverly sneaked in modern conveniences up on this hill, to the point where Micky is no longer protesting. You know Micky is dark and ignorant? Let me tell you; we had to fight him to get the electricity."

Ace settled down in his chair to hear more. Myrtle didn't need much by way of conversation. She just needed a verbal indication that he was listening.

"Micky has always been like this." Myrtle huffed. "Our parents were not big on education. I was the only one in the batch who went to school and only because I lived with Mrs. Johnson, my Sunday School teacher who thought I had potential. She wanted me to be a nurse. Unfortunately, she died before I graduated from Titchfield. Without her help, I barely finished high school."

"I came back to the district and took care of the Bronson's. Their house is the one that your parents bought."

Ace nodded. "I remember that name."

"Good people." Myrtle nodded, "Mrs. Bronson left to go back to England when Mr. Bronson died. When they sold the house, I worked in Port Antonio at Trident Castle for years."

"Fascinating, Myrtle," Ace murmured. "How did Micky fare at that time?"

"He started working from age ten." Myrtle sighed. "The rest of the cousins, Micky, included had to work on the farm. The thirty acres has been in the family for generations."

"It's a lovely place," Ace said. "I admire Micky for its upkeep. I often wonder how he manages such a large farm and still manages to be my occasional gardener."

"He can't manage the farm anymore," Myrtle murmured, "Guy is the one in charge now, Micky is mostly retired." Myrtle chuckled. "He goes to your place to keep himself busy and because of memories. He doesn't even take any money from you. Guy warned him not to because he wasn't a real gardener."

Ace nodded. So it was back to Guy again who sounded like the patron saint of the Wiley's.

"I offered Micky money once," Ace sighed, "it didn't go well."

He switched the subject back to Guy.

"So why doesn't Guy stay here and work the land? Why is he working somewhere else? What's wrong with him?"

Ace fumbled for a chink in Guy's armor. "Is he lazy?"

"Lazy?" Myrtle cackled. "Good heavens, lazy and Guy can't be in the same sentence. He is the most industrious, hard-working, busy, productive..."

"I get it," Ace chuckled dryly, "enough with the adjectives."

"We are not supposed to have favorites," Myrtle smiled serenely, "but of all the grandnephews, Guy is our hands-down favorite."

Chapter Nine

Guy slipped into the back pews of the Christ United Church on Thursday night. He knew that was where he would find Lucia; he was visiting Portland just for her sake. Walter had given him, the lenses, brand new. They were still in the box, and he wanted to deliver them to her. His presence didn't go unnoticed.

Lucia was the children's choir director of the medium-sized church and Thursday was the practice time. She waved to him from the front. She was in a mustard dress and with a matching headband around her hair. As usual, she stood out in any setting.

Novalee slipped in beside him as the children went through their paces.

"Hey, Guy."

"Hey, Novalee," he murmured.

"Here to see your girlfriend?" Novalee winked at him conspiratorially. "Did you know that Lucia is giving me the cold shoulder?"

"No," Guy shrugged. "Maybe you two should work it out between yourselves and not involve anyone else."

"That's what my father said." Novalee sighed. "I think she is the one who overreacted. She should be the one wanting to work it out."

Guy yawned widely. "How long is this practice going to last? I am tired."

"Another ten minutes or so." Novalee looked put out that he had changed the subject. "I have to practice the children for a skit after this."

"Okay." Guy glanced at his watch and then folded his arms.

"Why do you like her?" Novalee asked after a brief moment of silence between them.

"Because she is beautiful inside and out," Guy said without missing a beat.

"I am beautiful inside and out." Novalee batted her eyes at him. "Like me instead."

Guy was about to slam Novalee with a well-placed insult, but he looked into her uncertain hazel eyes and saw her obvious quest for attention and his heart melted.

"It doesn't work like that, Nova." He shortened her name deliberately.

She straightened up in the bench and preened. "I bet that I could get you to like me just like that, though."

She snapped her fingers. "I am prettier than Lucia by far."

"Why would you think that?" Guy frowned.

Novalee pouted her pink lips and then flipped her braids over her shoulder. "Because I am light skinned, of course. I have the coveted complexion that all the men go crazy for. Lucia is dark."

Guy looked at Novalee in horror. "That's your low self-esteem talking, Novalee. You should get some help for that. And stop comparing yourself to other girls especially Lucia. Maybe I should have a word with the Bishop about this attitude of yours. Light dark, medium, skin who cares?"

"No, don't tell daddy!" Novalee said guiltily. "I am sorry I said it. I didn't mean anything by it. I was testing you to see if you are like one of those people, after all, two of my sisters are dark skinned my mother is dark. I am not a colorist or whatever. I am just restating what I know to be true of our society and the men in this district."

Guy squinted at her and then shook his head. "Maybe Lucia is right in giving you the cold shoulder. With friends like you who needs enemies."

Guy got up.

"No, wait!" Novalee stood up as well. "I am sorry, maybe I am a little jealous of Lucia. I am a mad cow!"

She said the last bit loudly just when the choir finished their last note. The whole church heard.

Lucia turned toward them and grinned. "Yes, you are a mad cow."

The children giggled. Lucia walked from the choir loft, her skirt swishing around her slim legs as she walked.

Novalee sighed. "Unfortunately, I am a cow, and I am sorry for what I said a couple of days ago about you at work."

Lucia nodded. "Apology accepted."

Novalee looked at Guy pleadingly not to repeat what she said, and he nodded his head slightly.

Lucia tucked her hand in his and smiled at him. "Guy, it's always a serious pleasure to see you."

Guy grinned, and they walked out of the church. He could feel Novalee staring at them as they exited the church doors and it niggled at him that probably he needed to warn Lucia about her so-called friend.

"Tell me about Novalee," Guy said after he handed her the lenses and she squealed loud enough to wake up the Rio Grande wildlife.

"Why?" Lucia frowned at him in the half dark.

"Just curious." Guy shrugged. "You two seem pretty opposite in personality."

"I used to see her around school with her friends. Everybody knew who Novalee Rochester was, she was the popular girl who was involved in everything, but it wasn't until fourth form at the school choir auditions that we actually spoke."

Lucia chuckled. "When she stepped onto the stage to audition we were expecting great things. She was Bishop Rochester's daughter and her sister Candice was a year before and had the voice of an angel. You've heard her sing?"

Guy nodded. "I have. She's really good."

"But Nova was horrible." Lucia shook her head. "She had a cold and was determined to crack some high notes. The choir mistress told her to come back, and she left the stage crying, tripped over a bag and collided in me. We both fell to the floor."

"Oh," Guy leaned on the van.

"We went to the bathroom to clean up, and we chatted. I didn't see her again until after she auditioned a second time, this time she sounded really good. We sang in the soprano section and hung out when her main friends weren't around. The truth is, we never really became close friends until she started working at Wiley Groceries and she moved to the valleys after the bishop's demotion to this church."

Guy nodded. "Okay."

"I haven't had many friends, my mother says poor people can't afford friends, I couldn't pay for gifts to birthday parties or invite anybody to our house." Lucia murmured. "Besides that, I think I am an introvert."

"I am the same." Guy laughed. "My brother Walter who is the complete opposite of me likes to point that out. I like spending time in the greenhouse talking to plants rather than people."

Lucia grinned. "What do you say to these plants?"

"Stuff." Guy shrugged. "I talk to them about this pretty girl I know in the valleys."

"Oh," Lucia raised a brow. "What about her?"

"How she may not be ready for a relationship and that we are at different stages of our lives. I am a homebody she is just ready to spread her wings."

Lucia widened her eyes and then gasped. "Guy! We are talking about me aren't we?"

"Of course," Guy said touching her cheek. "Who else?"

"Well, I think you are wrong about the homebody bit, I don't mind being anchored to one place, I just think I have been anchored to the valleys for too long, besides..."

"Lucia!" Ace was standing at the church steps looking at them disapprovingly.

Guy straightened from the van.

"There you are." Ace approached them briskly. "Your mother said you would be here tonight. Something about a choir practice."

Ace paused and then looked over at him, "Guy Wiley. How are you?"

"Good." Guy nodded. "You?"

"I am giving thanks." Ace smiled smugly and then looked over at his van. "How does that thing still run? It looks like it is on its last."

Guy patted the rusty vehicle. "Suzy is okay. Just some minor problems now and again. After I fiddle with her engine, she is good again."

Ace laughed. "You named her Suzy."

Guy nodded.

"I was missing you," Ace dismissed him effortlessly and turned to Lucia. "Have you eaten? We could go to dinner."

Lucia glanced at him guiltily. "I am hungry but..."

Guy stepped closer. "Myrtle cooked steamed cabbage and dumplings and you know she is heavy handed with the scotch bonnet pepper."

Lucia nodded. "That sounds great!"

Ace laughed derisively. "I was thinking of taking you to Sunset Palms; it's Thursday night grill night by the pool. I made reservations."

Guy sighed inwardly. Sunset Palms was a popular expensive restaurant mainly frequented by those who could afford it. Myrtle's cabbage and dumplings was going to get the dump, and he wouldn't blame her. It was on his list of places to try with her when he finally revealed that he wasn't as poor as he made out.

But Lucia turned to him instead and grinned. "I have a hankering for Myrtle's cabbage and dumplings. Sorry, Ace. Goodnight."

She walked around to the passenger side of the vehicle and sat down.

Guy was almost as stunned as Ace looked.

****

"I can't believe she brushed me off like that," Ace said out loud. He laughed harshly. "Who chooses cabbage and dumplings over a gourmet meal at one of the most exclusive hotels in Portland."

"Obviously Lucia!" Somebody grunted behind him.

He spun around. Novalee Rochester walked up to him and shook her head.

"I will never understand that girl. I am free though. I can tell the kids to go home. I just gave them the parts to the skit; it was never going to be a long practice anyway."

"I am no longer in the mood." Ace headed to his car.

"Wait!" Novalee walked behind him. "I can help you with Lucia. This is like a competition between you and Guy Wiley, isn't it?"

"I am not in a competition," Ace snorted. "Lucia is a free agent; she can do what she pleases."

"Ha," Novalee snorted. "I can't believe that you are giving up, leaving her to the mercy of Guy Wiley. He is a mere farmer. You are a doctor. In intelligence alone you have him beat, not to mention that he doesn't even have his own place to stay, he lives in a cottage on the farm where he works, and he has nothing to his name. The only thing he has going for him is his looks and trust me, Lucia is not the only girl he likes. He likes me too, tells me so all the time."

"He does?" Ace frowned.

"Yes, Guy's a womanizer." Novalee drifted closer to Ace and then looked at his car. "It would be awful to waste that dinner reservation. I could tell you inside secrets about both Guy and Lucia."

Ace looked at her eager face and then sighed. "I guess it wouldn't hurt to know more about them, level the playing field so to speak."

Novalee nodded eagerly.

Chapter Ten

"Anything Myrtle cooks tastes like heaven," Lucia said wiping her plate clean. "No fancy restaurant can compare."

Guy chuckled. "I still can't believe that you ditched the doctor for me."

"It wasn't hard." Lucia smiled. "He laughed at your vehicle. I know what it feels like for people to look down on you because you are low on resources. I hate an entitled attitude."

Guy nodded. "I hear you."

"Do you people want anything else?" Myrtle poked her head around the door. "I have lemonade and Micky's beer."

"Lemonade please." Lucia nodded eagerly. "You do lemonade better than anyone I know, that beer tastes a bit too 'mediciny' for me."

"Your lemonade please." Guy nodded. "It is the right combination of tart and sweet."

Myrtle chuckled heartily. "Lucia and Guy, very good for

the ego."

"You are too modest." Guy smiled. "When is Uncle Micky coming home?"

"Around midnight," Myrtle snorted. "They have a nightly domino tournament at George's shop. Micky is on a winning streak, and all of the men in the neighborhood are trying to beat him. When he starts losing, I guess he'll start coming home earlier."

"At least he is not drinking," Guy said and winked at Myrtle. "Thank you for convincing him to make his own beer."

Myrtle nodded. "No problem."

She served them the lemonade and then left them on the veranda. It was a full moon, and the moonlit trees looked silvery below them. It was so bright, Lucia could see the river. The water was still, not even a ripple.

"You know this is my favorite view of the valleys." She looked across at Guy, "I think Myrtle and Micky are blessed."

"I think so too," Guy said. "When I was younger I used to come out here and look down at the view at nights. I don't remember what I was thinking about; I just stared at the river fixatedly."

"Myrtle used to run me to bed and murmur that I was a very strange child."

Lucia chuckled. "I can picture you, quiet, reserved, staring in one spot. It would probably freak me out too as an adult."

"I didn't just stare at the river. Some nights Uncle Micky would join me, and the two of us would stare at the stars in the sky."

"Kindred spirits." Lucia chuckled.

"Sometimes he would tell me stories." Guy grinned. "I have no idea if some of them are even true or tall tales from a fertile imagination. All I can say is that the people in the neighborhood are pretty colorful."

"Tell me some," Lucia said stretching out in her chair.

"Oh goodness," Guy muttered. "The most scandalous one of all was about Celia Jackson."

"Jackson!" Lucia looked at him sharply. "Any relation to Ace?"

"His mother." Guy chuckled. "Micky allegedly had an affair with her. He was their gardener in the early days. He only works for Ace now because I think in his own way he wants to get close to him."

Lucia rounded her eyes in horror. "What are you saying?"

"I am saying that Ace Jackson senior was always away, he had his private practice and worked at the hospital and Celia was lonely. She is from around here you know, she thought being a doctors wife would be different, but Ace senior forced her to give up her job, she was a nurse, and the lady was bored out of her skull. So I guess she distracted herself with Micky.

"Micky was a virile, handsome gardener in his prime."

Lucia gasped. "They had sex?"

"Repeatedly, according to Micky," Guy said. "He is under the impression that Ace and the second son, Deuce, may be his. Apparently, they only stopped the affair when Ace senior found out about it and moved his family from the district. That is why Ace senior won't ever come back to Portland. He even left the practice in the town. It was a thriving practice back then, you know. The man just upped and left it."

"I can't believe this," Lucia laughed. "You can't be serious."

"Micky was only half drunk when he told me." Guy grinned, "Who knows? Anything can be true when Micky is crying in his rum. According to him, Celia was his one great love."

"Wow." Lucia shook her head. "Double wow again. I can totally imagine Micky being hot. He is still a handsome man in his seventies. He has those sexy Wiley eyes."

Guy chuckled. "He is okay."

"So you are related to Ace Jackson?" Lucia giggled. "I can't believe it. He would be Ace Wiley, your cousin if he were given the right surname."

"I don't know about that." Guy shrugged. "As I said, Micky was half drunk. And Ace looks nothing like us."

"Except for the eyes," Lucia whispered. "The eyes are a dead give away! Now I know why Ace seemed so familiar when I just met him! It was the eyes!"

"I guess he has the same shaped eyes, but that is not an indicator that Micky was telling the truth," Guy said. "Besides, he could easily be related to Ace senior. Maybe Celia doesn't even know who the father is and she may never want to find out."

"It sounds like my family," Lucia murmured, "except there is no mistaking that I am a Wray. It still bothers me that I have two sisters and we don't talk. My oldest sister Sherene, when she comes into the supermarket, she would never come to my register."

"The second one, Shelly smiles at me all the time but she doesn't say a word."

"Not to mention their mother, ugh, she looks at me like she smells something bad and my father is the worst of them all, he avoids me like I would give him lice."

"One time I went into the store to buy a lock, and he was at the cash register. He rang up my sale and acted as if I were a total stranger."

"Wow," Guy murmured. "I think it is a mix of guilt and shame, you know. Guilt that he stepped out of the marriage, shame that you are around to point out his guilt."

"I guess." Lucia frowned. "Not every man is like that. Your father wasn't like that was he?"

"Oh no." Guy smiled faintly, "Joseph Wiley loved his family to a fault. In our case, we got more from him because he was always with us. He married Jennifer because of the supermarket and the promise he made to her father to run it after he died, but he had always loved my mother."

"Lucky you," Lucia sighed, "you had your father's love."

"Yes I did," Guy murmured. "I would never do what your father did to you. I couldn't. It is not in me to ignore a child of mine, ignore my flesh and blood. I couldn't watch and do nothing while he or she struggles. Never. Not knowingly. I don't care what goes down in my relationships. My child would be priority; it's the only way to do it."

Lucia smiled. "I knew that would be your response. Some kid will be lucky to have you as their dad."

Guy chuckled. "I would prefer to have that child or children in a stable relationship where the mother is my wife, and we are truly partners. That's why I have never been promiscuous."

"How not promiscuous have you been?" Lucia asked seriously.

"Oh boy," Guy murmured, "she asked the question."

"So?" Lucia sat up and looked at him fiercely. "Answer!"

"I am not a virgin," Guy said. "I had my first sexual encounter right here in this neighborhood."

Lucia felt a shaft of jealousy grip her. "My mother said country girls are easy and that's why I shouldn't even think about it."

"Your mother is the queen of generalizations." Guy chuckled. "Anyway, I have had two long-term relationships. The first one was in college; it ended when she left Jamaica. The second one was messy."

"Strawberry type of girl?" Lucia murmured.

"No, not really." Guy sighed. "I realized I loved someone else. I ended it. I realized that I couldn't cause her any more pain. She was thinking of wedding bells and marriage, so I made a clean cut. She is now engaged to someone else, and she says she is happier now than she had ever been with me. So, I guess it worked out for her."

"You love someone?" Lucia almost couldn't get the words past her hoarse throat.

"Yes." Guy turned his head and looked at her. "I do, for a long time. So what about you, how not promiscuous have you been?"

"I have never kissed someone." Lucia's head was still reeling from Guy's declaration that he loved someone. "I am still a virgin and will be until I get married. I am not compromising on that, and I don't care if anybody finds it old-fashioned and ridiculous."

Guy smiled. "You sound angry at me. I didn't say anything. I think it is admirable."

"You might just be the only one." Lucia sighed, "the word virgin is taboo these days."

"Nonsense." Guy murmured, "if more women in the neighborhood thought like you, then there wouldn't be as many fatherless children running around this place."

"I won again!" Micky announced loudly as he entered the house. "The undisputed heavyweight domino champion. I can take anyone. I am king."

"What time is it?" Guy looked at his watch and groaned. "It is after twelve. I have to drop you home."

Lucia got up and stretched. "It was nice hanging with you, Guy."

"The pleasure was all mine." Guy got up as well. "Let us exit swiftly before Micky starts describing his domino moves."

"I am the champion!" Micky said excitedly as they exited the front door.

"We heard." Guy chuckled. "Now go and get some sleep."

"Too excited to sleep, Micky said looking between him and Lucia. "I will wait up until you take Lucia home. I need to discuss my moves."

Guy sighed. "Okay, fine but do not wake up Myrtle."

"Nah," Micky sat down on the veranda. "I'll wait on you. You want my flashlight?"

"No, it's a full moon." Guy looked up at the sky. "The place is well lit."

"You know what they say about the full moon?" Micky cackled. "It's mating time."

"Micky," Lucia chastised him.

"You didn't know?" Micky feigned shock, "the moon cycles affect the human race in ways we don't realize especially since most of you have gone modern. You don't realize the power of the lunar cycles. You with your electric lights and your fancy appliances."

"Don't encourage him," Guy whispered in her hair. "Say goodnight and let us leave."

"Night Micky," Lucia said obediently.

"Night Miss Lucia," Micky cackled. "We'll talk about this another time."

They heard a cock crow in the distance; the silvery moonlight made everything look like a homogenous shadow in the dark. It was a typical Rio Grande night.

"Perfect night for a stroll." Guy looked over at Lucia. They were walking so closely their hands were touching.

"It is nice." Lucia inhaled, "I don't come out at night, and when I do I am always hurrying to get home. I didn't know I was missing a whole other world out here."

Guy pointed at a spider web on a banana leaf. Where the light hit it, it looked like glittering silver.

"Silver spider webs," Lucia whispered.

She sniffed the air. "And the scent of jasmine."

Guy nodded. "Micky planted several plants around the house because he says it relaxes him and makes him feel happy. And technically he is right. The jasmine plant has a pleasing and uplifting effect on the mind, and its scent actively fights depression. It makes people feel happy and potentially awakens romantic feelings."

Guy glanced at her. "Aren't you feeling romantic, right about now?"

Lucia chuckled. "Maybe."

"Let's see," Guy stopped and turned to her. He cupped her cheeks and ran his fingers across her skin lazily.

"How about now?"

"Most definitely." Lucia nodded.

Guy smiled, he looked as if he was debating going further.

Lucia inhaled shakily. Do it, do it, her heart was racing. Her lips felt dry, so she licked them.

He bent his head and captured her lips in a devouring kiss. From that first instant of contact, Lucia was electrified.

The flick of his tongue exploring the tender interior of her mouth made her jerk in shock and gasp.

Her hands came up to clutch at his thick hair. He crushed her to him, and she surrendered with enthusiasm. Excitement clawed at her body, and she wondered where her resolve was to remain a virgin until marriage.

She had never been kissed like this before. She had never been kissed before.

Guy dragged his mouth from hers and stared down at her intently. "The power of jasmine."

"No," Lucia shook her head, "I don't think so. I think it is just you."

"We'll have to test your theory," Guy said as they continued down the hill.

They stopped to kiss every two minutes on the twenty-minute walk to her house.

And then they stopped at her gate. The veranda light was on; she knew her mother was still up. Aretha didn't sleep until she was home.

Guy kissed her on her forehead. "Just in case your mother is looking."

"Will I see you tomorrow?" Lucia clutched his shirt. She was reluctant to let him go.

"No." Guy shook his head, "I have to leave at the crack of dawn. I just stopped by to bring you your lenses. Goodnight sweet Lucia, this night was unforgettable. I won't be around this weekend. I have been putting off some stuff I need to do."

Lucia nodded jerkily. "Sure. Yes, tonight was magical. I think I am dreaming."

"This is reality," Guy hugged her one last time, and they stood like that for what felt like hours.

"Sweet dreams," he said and released her.

He watched her as she went inside and then she watched as he walked off until she couldn't see him anymore. She wished that she could go with him and never look back.

"Lucia, that you?" Aretha asked groggily breaking into Lucia's wishful thinking.

"Yes mom," Lucia whispered. "I went to practice and then went with Guy to Micky's place."

And then he kissed me! Again and again and again.

She felt different. She felt as if her eyes were opened. She felt exhilarated. She couldn't sleep now.

"Guy Wiley!" Aretha snorted, getting up out of the settee.

"I am too sleepy to argue."

And Lucia was too spaced out to listen. She glided to her room as if she were on cloud nine.

Chapter Eleven

Ace and Novalee arrived at the beautiful Sunset Palms in the San San area of Portland. There was a resident live band playing classic Bob Marley and the Wailers, *Don't Rock My Boat*. The hostess seated them in an intimate spot at the poolside.

"Lucia is missing out," Novalee said looking around. "Her loss my gain."

Ace wasn't exactly feeling as philosophical. He was still fuming. He had underestimated Guy Wiley's pull on Lucia.

On the bright side, Novalee wasn't bad company. She chatted about herself a lot. He didn't have to contribute much to the conversation. A nod here and a grunt there and Novlee enthusiastically told him her life story. He knew about her third-place beauty pageant place in the parish competition, her father's unfortunate demotion, her four sisters and their various quirks, and her ambitions to be a clothing designer.

They were on the main course of grilled snapper before

Ace realized he wasn't having a terrible time with Novalee.

He had to admit she was entertaining and quirky. In all of her ramblings, he realized that she didn't know much about Lucia and she was even vaguer about Guy.

"Tell me about Lucia's high school boyfriends," he said when Novalee seemed to run out of commentary.

"None." Novalee shook her head. "Lucia was not very popular in school. She mostly kept to herself. When we became friends in fourth form, she was all about studying and the school choir."

Ace nodded. "That's good."

"Not that the boys didn't try." Novalee chuckled. "There was this one boy who threatened to kill himself if she didn't go to the fifth form dance with him."

"And did he kill himself?" Ace asked.

"No," Novalee shrugged, "someone else took pity on him. Lucia never went to the dance. She had nothing to wear. Not going never seemed to bother her, so I invited her over to my house when I was getting ready to let her get a feel for it."

"I see," Ace murmured. "You wanted to rub her face in it."

"No." Novalee gasped, "I offered her a dress, but she refused it. She didn't want to see me get ready either."

Novalee frowned. "Come to think of it, that was the year that Guy Wiley was missing. I think he went to Canada to work or something."

"He has been in her life that long?" Ace frowned.

"Yep." Novalee nodded. "If he was around, I am sure that Lucia would have gotten a dress. You know, if I didn't know better I would think that Guy Wiley has something to do with the Farm Help Society."

"The Farm Help Society?" Ace raised an eyebrow.

"Yes, the mysterious charity that built Lucia's family house and sends them groceries every week and buys clothes and shoes for the family. I mean they get a whole barrel of stuff from America every year. Some really nice things. Lucia owns several Jimmy Choo shoes and handbags, and she doesn't even appreciate it."

"Is that so?" Ace murmured. "I never really took note of stuff like that."

"Well, know this, if the Farm Help Society wanted to help me out I would not refuse it," Novalee said enviously. "I borrowed a blue blouse from Lucia last year, and when she gave it to me, I saw that it was pure silk, not imitation silk. I was shocked."

"So the charity is generous," Ace said sitting back in his chair, "how would Guy Wiley be involved?"

"I don't know." Novalee narrowed her eyes. "I can't make a connection. I wonder if his brothers, the rich ones are the Farm Help Society."

"The owners of Wiley Corp?" Ace raised an eyebrow.

"It would make sense," Novalee waited until the waiter had served bread pudding and ice cream for dessert before she continued. "I theorized that Myrtle told them about Lucia's family and then they helped."

"It's a reasonable assumption," Ace said contemplatively.

Novalee frowned. "I work for them too; surely they could send me some Jimmy Choo shoes. I could write to head office and tell them I live in the valleys and I am in need of shoes."

Ace chuckled. "Are you?"

"No, not in need just in want," Novalee grunted. "But Lucia doesn't need stuff anymore, but every year, like clockwork, she gets a new wardrobe."

"Do you think Guy is behind this and Lucia knows that is why she is so loyal to him?" Ace asked contemplatively. "It would explain a lot of things about her attitude to him."

"She claims that she doesn't know who is behind the Farm Help Society." Novalee snorted. "I can't see Guy doing it. He might know who is behind it. I don't know if he speaks to his brothers. Did you hear that Guy's father killed his mother?"

Novalee leaned toward him conspiratorially. She had finished devouring her dessert with gusto.

"Really?" Ace leaned back in his chair, nursing his drink.

"No, wait it was his father's wife that killed the mother," Novalee sighed, "I keep getting the story mixed up. Anyway, Wiley Groceries belongs to Guy's brothers from the wife. I guess Guy had to make a living somehow, so he became a farmer. That sucks. If I had brothers as rich as he has I would be asking them for a piece of the pie."

"Or maybe he did, and Lucia is the beneficiary." Ace offered.

"That would be something else," Novalee tapped the table. "I always thought Guy was just a poor farmer. There is more to Guy than meets the eye. I don't understand why he would drive that ugly van if he can do better."

Ace shrugged. "Some people just like old vehicles, it could be as simple as that. I doubt that Guy is as destitute as we think. Isn't Guy the person behind Micky Wiley's coffee farm? That farm is huge."

"No, that can't be it" Novalee shook her head, "I know several coffee farmers and they are not rich."

"He works elsewhere too. Do you know where that is?" Ace asked.

Novalee wrinkled her nose. "No, it is supposedly somewhere in the St. Andrew hills. He is a foreman there or something."

"Farmer versus doctor." Ace laughed humorlessly. "The farmer might win."

"Lucia has more sense than that." Novalee grinned. "You

don't have to worry about that."

"Farmers are the backbone of this society." Ace grunted. "Without farmers, there would be no other profession. What would we eat? I don't think him being a farmer is a disadvantage if anything it is a major plus in his case. Lucia will never go hungry if she is with him."

"Mmm," Novalee sighed. "You have your own house and car and practice. You have a lot more to offer."

"Means nothing." Ace shook his head. "If there is nothing bad about Guy, I am not even in contention here. Even a blind person can see that."

"Let me see." Novalee tapped the table searching for something bad to say about Guy. Ace's heart sunk.

She knew nothing.

Then Novalee snapped her fingers. "I know! He grew up with his uncle Micky, or at least he spent summers with him. Have you spoken to Micky? He is crazy, which means Guy probably has a touch of it, he is Micky's nephew."

Ace shook his head. "Micky is a brilliant man who knows more about plants than most botanists. Guy growing up with him is not a disadvantage. Yes, Micky has various conspiracy theories, and he can sometimes come across as slightly unhinged, but you know what, I like him, and maybe Lucia likes him too. She visits them a lot.

"I thought you had something solid, Novalee. Like how many girls have Guy gotten pregnant? Is he a cheater? That kind of thing."

"Oh," Novalee worried her bottom lip and then her eyes lit up.

"What?" Ace leaned forward.

"I could seduce him, and then you'd get all of Lucia's attention."

"I wouldn't ask you to do something like that. This is

not a soap opera. This is real life. I like things to happen organically." Ace looked at her, "besides, say you manage to seduce Guy, what is in it for you?"

"I want to see my friend, happy and settled," Novalee said piously. "That's all."

"And?" Ace raised an eyebrow, "somehow, you don't strike me as a selfless kind of person."

"Well," Novalee pouted, "I can be selfless and nice."

"I am sure of it." Ace nodded, "but in this case, you would want something. What is it?"

"Pay for an apartment in Port Antonio and my bills for a year so that I can escape my family. That is all," Novalee said in a rush, "be my Farm Help Society, it's not a bad deal. In the end, you will get your precious Lucia and Guy, well, he will have me. I am not even asking for Jimmy Choo shoes."

Ace tapped the table. He could pay for her apartment and bills; it wouldn't dent his finances one bit. He just wasn't sure that Guy would succumb to Novalee.

It wasn't just looks, they looked very different, but both were pretty girls. It had to do with their personalities.

Lucia was a sweet person, soft like marshmallow on the inside; Novalee, on the other hand, was like hard candy all over. One bite and you could break your teeth.

Novalee needed some softening first before she could make anybody a good girlfriend or wife. On the other hand, if Guy allowed himself to be seduced by Novalee, it was his loss, and it meant that his judgment was off.

He held out his hand to shake Novalee's. "It is a deal."

Chapter Twelve

"**Y**ou are cordially invited to the Chamber of Commerce ball, next week Thursday," Aretha said as soon as Lucia walked through the door Monday after work.

"What's that?" Lucia asked, pointing to a brightly wrapped gift basket and the card in her mother's hand.

"From your doctor friend," Aretha said. "Just reading the card because I am nosey. Can you imagine Lucia, the Chamber of Commerce ball? Oy, I am so excited."

Lucia sat on the settee and closed her eyes tiredly. "I already signed up to serve there. Today!"

"Serve there?" Aretha raised her eyebrows haughtily. "No can do. You have to go as a guest."

"I don't want to go with Ace," Lucia said weakly, "I am getting serious with Guy."

Aretha opened her eyes widely and stood up. "Okay, now see here. I am tired of talking about Guy and Ace and who will give you a better future. You won't listen, and I am sick of it, but I don't care about that right now. What I care about is you going to this ball. It is important to me."

"How?" Lucia asked confused.

"Because Chilton Wray will be there." Aretha nodded. "Yes, your father who denies that you exist. You are going to show up at the doctor's side, and you are going to look like a million dollars, and you are going to make your deadbeat father wish he had gotten to know you."

Lucia straightened up on the couch. Her mother had a point. It stung to have a parent in the same town who ignored her though she passed his hardware store every day. If he happened to see her, he would look right through her as if she didn't matter, as if he didn't help to conceive her. It was as if he didn't know that at one point they were living in the almshouse, just a street over from his store.

She liked what her mother was thinking, but she would have to go on a date with Ace, and she was 99.9% sure that something had shifted in her relationship with Guy.

She had concluded that she was the one he loved. She was the reason he ended the relationship with his girlfriend. The facts were there, and they didn't lie, Guy made his way to Bowden Pen ever so often so that he could see her. She felt his desire for her in their kisses.

But, he wouldn't be back until the weekend. He wouldn't know that she went to the ball. The idea was to go to the ball with Ace, not as a date, but to cause her father to regret. That was all.

It was doable.

"I don't have anything to wear," Lucia murmured. "At least not ball worthy dresses."

"Don't worry about it," Aretha said, "I will take care of that."

****

Ace was waiting for her after work on Tuesday. He waved to her when she exited the building. He was talking on his cell phone, and when she approached him, he grinned, "My lady, I am formally inviting you to the ball, and your mother pointed out that you do not have a dress. So, we are going dress shopping."

Lucia frowned. "I thought she was going to make something."

Ace widened his eyes in consternation. "Don't take this the wrong way, Lucia, but your mother is not a fashion designer, correct?"

"Correct, but she is more than capable as a seamstress," Lucia said. "She has made me things before."

Mainly from old curtains, but she was not going to say that aloud. Besides, she felt weird to go shopping with Ace. She didn't want him doing things for her. She didn't want to feel beholden.

Why had she never felt that way about Guy? He helped her family all the time, and she had never felt awkward about it.

"Come on," Ace said easily, "we can do this, this is not charity, trust me. It is a necessity. Besides, you'll love shopping with me; I am the most patient male shopper in the world."

Lucia didn't argue further. Visions of her showing up at the ball in something like the boxy, billowy dresses her mother used to sew from the curtains propelled her into the vehicle.

Besides, she hadn't forgotten the real reason why she was attending the ball. It was an opportunity to show her father that she had thrived despite his neglect.

She reassured herself of that fact through the entire hour and fifteen minutes of trawling through the clothing boutiques in Port Antonio, but she couldn't help feeling as if she was using Ace and that her mother had trapped her somehow.

She finally found a dress. It was a peacock print with sequins that fit her as if it were custom made.

Ace insisted on getting her accessories as well. He was charming and patient and eventually had her relaxing with him.

He had a sense of humor too. He insisted that they go to Sunset Palms for dinner because they had not gone for their date. She found that she couldn't say no this time, especially since he had been so kind to her.

It wasn't a bad meal at all. She loved the atmosphere and the company and realized that she was being charmed out of her reluctance to let her guard down.

"Why don't you have a cell phone?" Ace asked when he dropped her home. "I have a signal at my house, albeit a very weak one. You should have an even better reception here. We could keep in touch."

He pulled out his cell phone and checked it. "I am getting one bar here."

"When my brother stops by this weekend I'll ask him to bring one for me," Lucia said hurriedly. She didn't want Ace to be buying her a cell phone.

"Your brother, huh?" Ace asked suspiciously.

"Yes, my brother." Lucia frowned. "He works in St Ann. He has a company vehicle, and he is coming by this weekend. He'll get me a cell phone. I'll give you the number when I get it."

She exited the car and then spun around. "I am tired of being a charity case, Ace. I want you to understand that."

"I understand," Ace said, frustration bubbling in his voice. "You are saying you can't be bought. You are fiercely independent and proud except when it comes to Guy Wiley and the Farm Help Society and your brother and everybody else but me. You know, you have nothing to prove to me. I get it; you don't want me for my money. I do get it."

Lucia glared at him and then threw the shopping bags back into the car. "That's it. I am not going to the ball with you."

"Come on Lucia," Ace said exasperatedly, "I am sorry. I had no intention of saying that. Why are you punishing me? I am a man. I like you. I want to give you gifts. I hate when you make a two-bit production out of everything. I don't think you are a gold digger, okay. Nor do I think I am better than you because I have a medical degree and practice medicine. I am a mere country doctor courting a woman who is more prickly than a cactus. My only sin is suggesting that you get a cell phone. That's all."

She was acting unnecessarily prickly. Lucia reluctantly smiled and took out the bags from the back seat where she had unceremoniously thrown them. "I'll give you my cell phone number when I get it."

Ace nodded. "And you are coming to the ball?"

"Sure." Lucia nodded. "Thank you for the invite."

"Now that's better," Ace whispered and winked at her.

Chapter Thirteen

Lucia felt like a princess when she stepped into the living room two days later. She had never dressed up to go anywhere before now, except for church and that didn't count because her church clothes were not by any stretch of the imagination, fancy.

She spun around and looked in the mirror. Her skin glowed, her eyes sparkled, she looked different like she had a major makeover when she hadn't. She had asked one of the girls at the supermarket who always had flawless makeup to tell her what to do.

Kami had looked at her and shook her head. "You don't need it. I'd kill to have your glow; your skin is flawless— looks like you already have on makeup. With some lip gloss, your lips are already that deep red, and maybe a little mascara you will look amazing."

She had done what Kami said, and now here she was, looking fancier than she had ever seen herself. She carried her camera outside to her mother who looked as if she was going to cry.

"Oh, Lucia, you look so pretty," Aretha blubbered, "like a Barbie doll. And your hair! It has gotten so long!"

Lucia rolled her eyes. "Mom, you saw my hair yesterday!"

"It was in a ponytail, not out and big and curly. You look different." Aretha blinked rapidly. "This is how you should look all the time."

"Dressed for a ball?" Lucia snickered.

"No," Aretha said exasperated, "you should look glamorous. You should live a glamorous life."

Lucia shook her head. "Oh no. Not this again. Take my picture, pretty please. I'll show you what to do. We should take it outside by the hibiscus it has on a couple of yellow blooms, it will make a nice contrast to this dress."

Aretha nodded. "Oh yes."

Lucia posed and preened before the hibiscus bush until Ace came to pick her up.

"Wow Lucia," he said stepping out of the car, "you clean up well."

"Thank you," Lucia smiled, "so do you."

"Let me take a picture of the two of you," Aretha said eagerly. "Has anyone ever told you that you both look good together?"

Lucia looked at Ace, and he looked at her, and they laughed. Her mother was so obvious it was painful.

"No mom," Lucia muttered, "you are the first."

"Yes, we do look good together." Ace winked at her.

And for a minute, after he winked, Lucia could see a slight resemblance to Micky Wiley and even Guy. They had the same shaped eyes.

And since Guy had told her that little piece of gossip, it wouldn't leave her head.

She looked at Ace a little bit too long, and his eyes softened. "Are you ready?"

"Yes, sure." Lucia nodded. "Bye, mom."

"Bye dear," Aretha said, looking like she had just won the lottery or something.

"She is right to be hopeful," Ace said when they drove off, "I am more than besotted with you, Lucia."

Lucia cleared her throat. "Ace..."

"I know," Ace smiled at her, "you like Guy Wiley. After all, you chose him over me the other night. I get it. He seems like the adventurous type with a happy go lucky air to him.

"But do you really know Guy? He is good-looking yes. A man like him is popular with women. He'll always be a source of problems for you; you'll always wonder about him."

"Guy is not like that," Lucia said crossly. Ace didn't respond to that.

"And let's face it, he doesn't seem to be financially stable or has any plans. What are his future plans, Lucia?"

To plant more mango trees. Lucia thought.

She glared at Ace instead. "I am not going to discuss Guy."

"I am just saying; I heard from a reliable source that he likes someone else."

Lucia gasped. "No."

"Yes," Ace grimaced. "I didn't want to bring this up, but I thought you should know. And to let you know that by contrast, I don't like anybody else, I don't just like you; I love you. And to lay it out on the line, I'll just let you know that my future plans are to marry you and we move out of the valleys."

Lucia closed her eyes. She didn't know how to react or what to think.

"Ace this is a lot."

"I know," Ace smiled, "but I just thought you should know. I am done with moving slowly with you. Today is the beginning of a different Ace."

****

The ball was just what she had expected; the venue was gorgeous, the Jamaica Palace Hotel had a beautiful view of Turtle Harbor, the attendance was a virtual who's who of the business community.

There was a light breeze and weak sunlight that cast a golden glow over the gathering.

She spotted her father at the same time that he did her.

He stopped moving. She could see him widen his eyes and then freeze. Their eyes met and held, hers with glittering triumph, his with fear or was that regret?

She had no idea. They lost the moment. His wife hooked her hands in his and dragged him away to talk to somebody. She glanced at Lucia coldly before pulling her husband away.

"You look so gorgeous that a man literally stopped in the middle of the crowd and gawped at you and his jealous wife is pulling her husband away," Ace murmured beside her.

"That's just my father and his wife."

A passing waiter stopped with drinks, but Lucia's hands were too unsteady to hold it. She had made her presence known to her father; he had seen her and was shocked. Mission accomplished.

So why was it that her hand had a tremor, and she felt slightly breathless?

"Your father?" Ace looked at her curiously. "Really?"

"Yes, that is Chilton Wray of Wray Hardware." Lucia frowned. "We have the same last name you know. My mother made sure of that. She thought that if she did that he couldn't deny my existence, after all, we live in the same town and we resemble each other a great deal. I look more like him than his other children."

"Ah," Ace nodded.

"But it makes him uncomfortable that I exist, and he does pretend that my mother had an abortion." Lucia inhaled raggedly and then smiled at Ace. "And you know what, I really couldn't care less."

Ace placed a hand in the small of her back. "Usually, when people say that they don't care, they care a whole heap more than they are letting on."

Lucia sighed. "You are probably right."

"I know I am right," Ace whispered. "If it makes you feel better, my father and I are not exactly the closest either. I grew up in a two-parent household, my parents love each other, but sometimes I feel blanked out by my father. I can't quite put my fingers on why.

"We never really gelled, my dad and I. As the oldest of three boys I sometimes get the feeling that I am the odd one out. I was quite surprised when he sent me here to wrap up his business and to close the house. I used to think that he couldn't trust me with anything.

"I was named after him, but somehow, I don't feel like a junior. I feel like an interloper. I am just saying, that this kind of thing happens in seemingly perfect families too."

Lucia cleared her throat. "Oh, Ace. Maybe there is a reason for that. Perhaps you could talk to your mother about it.

"My mother, I do talk to her about it," Ace shook his head. "She thinks I am overreacting."

Lucia looked at him and for a moment was tempted to tell him about Micky Wiley and the affair with his mother, but it wasn't her place.

It wasn't long before they were stopped by a few persons

who wanted to talk to Ace. He introduced her to them and pulled her close to him possessively, anchoring her at his side, sending the message that she was special. She didn't know what to think about it. She still had not worked out what she would do about her feelings for Guy. Maybe she should keep her options open.

She liked Ace. He was a good man. So what if they didn't have sizzling chemistry? Maybe her mother was right, and she had to think practically. Perhaps she needed to be sensible and see past Guy's good looks and kisses that made her forget where she was.

"Hey Lucia," Dominic Black, the supermarket manager, greeted her and then Ace.

Lucia suddenly felt shy and tongue-tied. She was not used to being in a social setting with her boss.

She hadn't even recovered from the greeting when a muscular, draw-dropping, handsome man came up to Dominic. He looked over at her and smiled.

"Lucia Wray?"

"Yes... er yes."

He smiled again. "My name is Walter Wiley. Nice to meet you."

They shook hands. Lucia knew her mouth was hanging open, but she couldn't close it. Not for anything. Somehow she wasn't picturing Guy's brother to look so different, maybe because Guy was so lithe and lean and looked biracial. This brother was a hunk. Even the tux couldn't conceal it. He was light skinned, had pink chiseled lips and a firm handshake.

"Can we talk?" Walter asked her while she stood there dizzily taking him in. "Privately."

Ace looked between the two of them. "Why?"

"Is it about the camera lenses?" Lucia finally found her voice. "I told Guy to tell you thank you."

"You are related to Guy?" Ace asked.

"He is my brother." Walter nodded.

Ace reluctantly removed his hand from her waist and stepped back. Lucia followed Walter to the end of the walkway, near a tall potted palm.

"So you are Lucia?" Walter looked at her appreciatively. "I get it now."

"Get what?" Lucia frowned.

"The reason why Guy wanted the lens." Walter smiled. "He doesn't ask for much you know, will not ask for a thing for himself. Quite independent our Guy. It takes you to make him come out of his shell."

"Yes, he is independent." Lucia nodded. "Let me say thank you in person. I know they are expensive and one day when I..."

"Oh stop," Walter grinned, "I couldn't accept payment. As I said, Guy doesn't ask for much. It's nothing to give you the lens. I wanted to discuss something with you though other than that. Guy said that you have no place to stay when you come to Kingston in a month."

"That's right," Lucia nodded. "I haven't had the time to panic about that yet."

"Well then, you are in luck. There is an empty townhouse beside where I live. You are welcome to stay there."

"Wow," Lucia widened her eyes. "Thank you. But I wasn't planning to stay overnight anymore. I am taking my two weeks vacation and I..."

"Oh, staying for two weeks will be fine." Walter smiled. "As I said Guy doesn't ask for much. He also said that you would need a ride to the event and to get around town. My wife Aisha is happy to help. It will be summer holiday for her. She is a teacher, and she is looking forward to meeting you."

"Oh, thank you." Lucia nodded. "Thank you so much. You are all so kind."

Walter nodded. "It's not a problem."

He was accosted shortly after that by an incessant young lady from a newspaper and Ace found her before she could even say a proper goodbye.

"What was that about?" Ace asked pulling her away to the end of the patio.

"He offered me a place to stay when I go to Kingston for the wedding."

"Which wedding?" Ace frowned.

"My very first photo shoot," Lucia said excitedly. "I can't wait."

"You didn't tell me. If you had told me before, you could have stayed at my apartment," Ace mumbled. "It would be perfect. I could take some time off too. We could explore Kingston together."

"I don't know," Lucia lowered her voice when someone passed by them.

"You prefer to stay with Guy Wiley's family?"

"I just got the offer," Lucia said exasperation lacing her voice, "and Walter said it was a townhouse beside his. I wouldn't be staying with the family."

Ace looked unimpressed. "Let's change the subject. I don't want Guy Wiley to ruin my evening with you once more."

The live band played old hits through most of the evening. They left the venue to Fab 5's *All Night Party* with even the staidest people dancing on the floor. She had even spotted her father and his wife happily dancing along without a care in the world.

Lucia had never seen them in such a playful way. It dawned on her that they were human like everyone else. Maybe Chilton Wray's coping mechanism was to ignore her. He had stayed with his wife and had his family; her birth was just an unfortunate event that he was trying to ignore.

It was understandable on some level. It didn't stop his rejection from hurting her, but it was understandable.

Lucia sighed.

The need to prove herself to her father seemed so futile now.

She danced with Ace for two songs, but her heart really wasn't in it. She developed a headache and was relieved when Ace offered to take her home. The party was winding down anyway.

"It was fun," Lucia said when they were on their way home.

Ace had loosened his bow tie and unbuttoned the top two buttons on his shirt to be more comfortable.

"We should do it again." Ace grinned at her, "I see that you can dance. You need to do it more often."

"Me, dance?" Lucia chuckled. "I just go with the music, but it was fun."

"We would have plenty of opportunities to go out when we are in Kingston." Ace glanced at her. "We could be there as soon as you say the word."

"Which word?" Lucia fidgeted with the bracelet.

"Yes, I will marry you," Ace said simply.

Lucia swallowed. "Ace, I love someone else."

"Guy Wiley," Ace murmured, "Why do you love him? Have you ever thought about it? Is it his looks, his connections to money, his charm?"

"He is a genuine person, honest, kind, considerate and thoughtful. I have known him for years now. Guy is more than his looks. He never mentions his connections to money. It's not an issue for him. He is very independent.

"You know what his brother said to me this evening, Guy

doesn't ask them for anything, so when he asked Walter for the camera lens he was more than happy to give it!"

Lucia turned to Ace crossly, the seatbelt constricting her from turning fully to him in unhidden rage. "Guy is perfect just the way he is!"

"There is no such thing as a perfect guy." Ace grumbled. "Why did his parents have to name him Guy? Its just so oxymoronic...perfect and Guy. You are in fairytale mode with this man, Lucia."

Ace smirked. "Nobody is perfect and certainly not him. He is going to break your heart and shatter your trust in men. I can see it coming. I hope it is not too late for me."

"Ace I don't want to talk about this anymore." Lucia sat back in her seat and looked through the window.

Why was it that when she and Guy had walked through the countryside only a week ago, it had seemed so romantic and magical. It was the same conditions; the full moon cast everything in its silvery glow, yet she felt like decking him for talking rubbish.

"I know you are angry now," Ace said, "I know you think you have it right but trust me when the scales fall off and you see Guy for who he is, I'll be here. I love you enough for the both of us."

They reached at her house. Her brother's van was in the driveway, and most of the lights were on.

"So you got your phone?" Ace asked raising an eyebrow.

"Not yet." Lucia smiled, "but he has it with him. I think he stopped by to drop it off. He is working this weekend."

"Okay." Ace nodded. "Remember to give me your number and don't forget what I said. I will be here whatever happens."

"Nothing will happen." Lucia turned to Ace. "What you see is what you get."

Ace looked at her intently and then sighed. "Let me walk

you to the door."

He got out and came to her side of the car and opened it.

Lucia got out and almost stumbled in her heels.

Ace reached out an arm to steady her and then held her like that for a while.

"I will not give up on you so easily, Lucia," he whispered, "I'll ride out this infatuation."

Lucia stepped out of his arms. "Goodnight Ace, thank you for a lovely evening."

"Goodnight Lucia, it was my pleasure."

He followed her to the door and ran his fingers across her cheek in a light caress.

Lucia let herself into the house, a mass of uneven, confused feelings curling through her.

Chapter Fourteen

"**I** saw you with Ace yesterday," Novalee winked at Lucia. "You two were looking all loved up at the ball."

Lucia widened her eyes. "Loved up?"

"Yes," Novalee nodded. "He is really into you, isn't he? He can't take his eyes off you and all of that. I am jealous. How was the ball? They had me on kitchen duty. I had to wash a million plates."

Lucia looked around the break room; there were three more staff members huddled in a corner and eating lunch and talking among themselves.

She leaned toward Novalee. "It was okay, keep your voice down."

Novalee frowned. "Girl, it wasn't just okay. I helped clean up after dinner, and I could feel the money in the room. What's wrong with you and this low key 'It was okay'?"

"I am fine." Lucia looked at her plate. Usually, she took a subsidized lunch from Yum Yum cafe, but today she had her leftover dinner from yesterday that she hadn't eaten because of the ball.

It didn't look very appetizing. She had overheated it in the microwave. The stewed chicken was now rubbery and the rice crispy.

She hated to waste food. She closed the plate in disgust. It was no use. It wasn't edible.

Novalee pushed her plate over to her. "Have it. I am not hungry."

"Thank you," Lucia beamed at her friend. "I should be the one asking what's wrong with you? Usually, you eat like you are starving."

Novalee shook her head. "Nothing is wrong. Tell me about the ball."

"The ball?" Lucia shrugged. "The food was good. They had awards for businesses, Wiley Groceries got one. Dominic accepted it. Walter Wiley gave the keynote address. It was good. He is a very entertaining speaker."

"And drop-dead gorgeous," Novalee whispered. "All the girls in the kitchen were discussing him. Is he married, do you know?"

"Yes, he is married." Lucia shrugged. "I spoke to him. He seems nice."

"Look at you, rubbing shoulders with the rich and handsome," Novalee said enviously. "I would pay to be in your shoes right now."

"Why, I thought you said nothing was wrong." Lucia raised an eyebrow.

"Well...I don't even want to think about it." Novalee looked around nervously, "I think I am late."

"Late for what?" Lucia tucked into the food with unrepentant glee. It tasted even better than usual.

"Late." Novalee almost screeched. She snapped her fingers

in front of Lucia's face. "Concentrate."

"Oh," Lucia looked at Novalee in consternation, "as in pregnant? How? Who?"

"How?" Novalee lowered her voice, "the usual way, sex with no protection. I should have kept my virginity, but that horse already went through the gate from high school. Remember Jerry Long ?"

"Yes," Lucia frowned, "his parents own the electronics store downtown. I saw him at the ball too."

"Yup. That one." Novalee made a face. "I thought we had a thing. It turned out I was just a stand-in for my sister who he has always lusted after, the perv."

"So how did this recent thing happen?" Lucia asked confused.

"It was a couple of weeks ago. I needed a ride to go home. I saw him. We did it in his vehicle."

"Who is this he?" Lucia whispered.

"It doesn't matter." Novalee fidgeted, "I have just screwed up my life big time."

Lucia was suddenly not hungry anymore. "So it wasn't one of the men on your top list then?"

"Jeez no. If it were one of them I would be rejoicing," Novalee murmured. "Unfortunately, Dominic is off. I may have overestimated his attention, I go out of my way to say hello when I see him, but he is giving me the stink eye as if he wasn't the one who said he liked me. As for Ace, he is not interested. He obviously loves you without a doubt."

"So this person is a local, from the valleys?" Lucia asked fearfully.

"You could call it that." Nova shrugged. "He's mostly a visitor now. He works out of the parish."

Lucia swallowed her food with difficulty. "Say what?"

"I was standing at the junction waiting for a taxi, and he

stopped to give me a lift. We talked. He said he had always had a crush on me and was tired of not telling me how he felt. It was raining, we stopped at Jose Wales corner, we listened to romantic music, we started kissing, and one thing led to the other.

"I had low key liked him for years. He is fine after all, but oh goodness, I don't know what came over me. I was feeling low, I guess. I feel as guilty as ever, and now I am late."

"Are you serious?" Lucia asked hoarsely. "You are not pulling my leg here."

"No," Novalee bit her lip. "My parents are going to kill me. My father is going to kill me and then him."

"I'd say," Lucia whispered. "You are going to have to get married to save face or poor Bishop won't be able to show his face in the valleys again. He is always boasting about his golden girls and how pure they are."

Novalee winced. "I don't even know if this person genuinely likes me, we were lost in the moment. Marriage, I don't think he wants that."

"Tell me who it is," Lucia said earnestly.

"No." Novalee shook her head. "I can't. You will freak out."

Lucia frowned. "No, I won't."

"Oh yes, you will." Novalee nodded vigorously. "I can guarantee that you will have heart failure. It was a stupid, foolish mistake that was over in a couple of minutes and now I may be carrying his baby. This is unfair."

Lucia sat and watched her friend. A slow dread crept up her spine. The only person she would freak out about having sex with her friend would be Guy Wiley. If that happened a piece of her would die. Yes, it would.

"It isn't..." her voice trailed away faintly. If she asked and the answer was yes. What on earth would she do? How would she cope?

"I am going to have to move out of my parents home," Novalee said faintly. "He doesn't even have any money. I am way too pretty for this. I feel as if this is not the trajectory that my life should be on. There is a process, courtship, engagement, marriage and then baby. How on earth am I at baby, before courtship?"

She covered her face and then peeped through her fingers.

"Do you think the Farm Help Society would help me now? I am going to be destitute in a couple of months. Do you know how much babies cost? They are expensive, and they keep getting expensive the older they get."

Lucia didn't respond to Novalee at; first, dread still had her in its clutches. She belatedly heard the question as if Novalee was far away and not right in front of her. "I... er... don't know."

"Who's behind the Farm Help Society anyway?" Novalee asked. "Did you find out?"

"No. Myrtle said that they liked to help anonymously. I usually write to them and give it to Myrtle and then they would fulfill my requests."

"Myrtle Wiley?" Novalee narrowed her eyes. "She lives in that log cabin with her cousin Micky Wiley, for years and years, they don't go anywhere, they don't know anyone. How can she know of a secret society that help people?"

"I don't know," Lucia said grumpily. She pushed away her plate. "We have been too grateful for the help to be questioning the source."

Novalee sniffed. "I guess I am too nosy. Maybe I am not cut out to be a charity case.

Then she realized how condescending she sounded and her head snapped up and she looked at Lucia in horror. "No offense. I am not calling you a charity case."

"It is what it is," Lucia said, tapping her fingers on the table. "If it weren't for the Farm Help Society I would be... who knows where? And you have called me a charity case before."

She glanced at her watch and then glared at Novalee dispassionately. "My break is over."

Novalee nodded. "I have a couple more minutes. I might hit the town, pick up a test, or maybe it is too soon to tell. It is barely a month."

"Aren't you going to tell me who your secret baby daddy is?" Lucia asked huskily.

Novalee shook her head. "I don't know if there is even a baby. When I do, I'll let you know."

"Not even a hint." Lucia's heart was doing a weird hop skip jump rhythm, and she was finding it difficult to breathe.

Novalee looked at her mutely and then sighed. "I am not saying a word until I know what the results say. I already told you it's not your doctor boyfriend. You shouldn't look so worried."

Lucia frowned. "I am not worried."

"And you can't breathe a word of this to anyone," Novalee lowered her voice. "I can't deal with any of this getting back to my father. Promise me."

"I won't breathe a word," Lucia said reluctantly.

Chapter Fifteen

"**L**ying lips are an abomination unto the Lord, and they that speak truly are his delight!" The Bishop was in fine form as he preached the message for youth week of prayer.

Lucia felt like it was not just her lips. Her whole mind was an abomination.

She had told Novalee that she was not worried about her potential baby daddy being Guy, but she was.

More than worried. It was a full week since the ball, and the conversation after with Novalee and she could not get it out of her head. Novalee didn't look pregnant but who looked pregnant at just a month's pregnancy?

She glared at her friend. She was sitting in the opposite pew from hers, sitting prim and proper with a tiny white hat perched jauntily on her head. Nodding and saying amen to her father's sermon like she was an attentive first daughter and not a loose-living hussy who had sex with a guy, in a vehicle.

A guy or her Guy? Lucia wondered feverishly.

"My girls don't lie to me," the bishop said breaking into Lucia's reverie, "they know to tell the truth, honesty is the best policy."

Lucia closed her eyes in rejection of the bishop's ridiculous utterances. He still thought Novalee was as pure as the driven snow. Nova probably lied to him every day.

Lucia worried her bottom lip. She couldn't continue like this. She had to ask Guy if he had sex with Novalee because Novalee was not saying.

She had to know though. If she didn't get this sorted out in her head, she was going to explode.

"Let us stand for prayer." The bishop's last few moments of warning flew right over her head. She was so lost in thought that she had not even responded; she belatedly realized that people were pairing up in twos to pray.

Nobody was sitting on her bench near the back, but she looked behind her for a partner anyway. She gasped when she saw Guy. He was sitting there dressed completely in black, looking like the handsome lead in one of those telenovelas that they played in the lunchroom at work. His long hair was gone. In its place was a thick swathe of tousled black curls.

He smiled at her slowly and then got up and came over. He stood so close to her she could feel his body heat.

"What happened to your hair?" She whispered.

"I donated it to the Cancer Society." Guy took her hands in his, "I do it every three years or so."

"That is so sweet," Lucia beamed at him, "I like it like this."

"My head feels lighter," Guy squeezed her hand. "Let us pray. I think a couple of people are giving us the side eye."

Lucia nodded. "Let us pray."

She didn't remember what she said to God. She was

silently asking for forgiveness when the service ended. Her pulse had been racing when Guy took her hand, and she had been busy inhaling his scent. Guy smelled good.

They greeted the bishop at the door after the meeting.

"Lucia Wray," Bishop Rochester beamed at her benevolently and then turned to Guy. "You know Lucia is one of my most exemplary young persons. She is a virtuous woman. Take heed Guy Wiley."

Guy nodded and smiled. "Well noted."

"And should be acted upon before she is snatched away by others who have also noted," the bishop said playfully.

Guy nodded solemnly. "I agree."

"Where is your vehicle?" Lucia asked when they walked through the church parking lot. There was a green pickup that she had seen Guy drive before.

"Suzy died on me the mechanic said she is only fit for the scrap metal heap." Guy looked unperturbed, "I borrowed the new vehicle from a family friend."

"I see," Lucia murmured, "may Suzy's parts rest in pieces."

"They won't." Guy shook his head, "they are going to melt her down and create something else."

"So the green van in the churchyard is your new Suzy?" Lucia laughed at him.

"No," Guy looked hurt. "You can't just bestow the name Suzy on a new vehicle. There can only be one Suzy. She was my ride or die. My stalwart friend through rain and storm. Besides, the green van is just a borrow. It will have no name."

"I see." Lucia chuckled. "Rain or storm though? I thought you had difficulty starting Suzy on a bright sunny day?"

"I prefer to focus on the positives," Guy said, "Suzy deserves fond memories."

Lucia bit her lip and looked at him. She wanted to ask him about Novalee so badly. It was on the tip of her tongue to blurt it out.

She cleared her throat instead.

Guy looked at her. "So what's up? Two whole weeks without seeing you was torture."

"I met your brother, Walter, at the Chamber of Commerce ball."

"I know, he told me." Guy sighed. "How was it, the ball?"

"It was good."

Guy was silent for several moments after that. "I was jealous."

He finally broke the silence. "I tortured myself with all kinds of scenarios when I heard that you went with Ace. I asked myself, does she realize that the other night was a turning point in our relationship? Does she realize that I can't play it cool anymore? Did she kiss him? Are they a couple now? Did I wait too long to make my move? Is she going to choose the doctor over me?"

"No we didn't kiss, no we aren't a couple, no you didn't wait too long to make a move and no I am not going to choose the doctor over you." Lucia stopped in the middle of the road. There was no traffic anyway.

"I don't think you should go out with him again or entertain him." Guy stopped a little before her. "My heart can't take it, okay."

"Okay," Lucia nodded. "I'll tell him that I am in a serious relationship with you now. We are official."

Guy nodded. "That's right."

"And this means that I have to get something off my head," Lucia sighed, "I can't stop thinking about this. Did you have sex with Novalee?"

"What?" Guy looked shocked.

"Did you?" Lucia asked again.

"No." Guy frowned. "Where did that come from?"

"I am not supposed to say anything about her situation. I just wanted to clear your name from the potential suspects." Lucia sighed, "Can I change the subject?"

Guy ran his fingers through his hair. "So Novalee is in the family way, and you assumed it was me?"

"No, she said the potential person was someone who doesn't live in the parish, he comes by for occasional weekends, and he gave her a lift. I don't know anybody else who fits that description but you."

"Really?" Guy asked. "I know a couple of people like that. Mostly all the construction workers in the area work out of the parish. Bob Jones, Carey Campbell, Lloyd Pennicook, that guy who works in St. Mary, that lives beside her and the..."

"Okay," Lucia inhaled, "I guess I was paranoid."

"I am not interested in Novalee."

They started walking again, and they passed George's shop. George was playing music as usual. He had an arsenal of reggae music that he played to entertain his patrons every night.

There were men at the two domino tables at his shop front and others in his bar. One man was in the corner dancing and hugging himself to Richie Spice's, *Groovin My Girl*.

"Nice lyrics." Guy chuckled as the man started moving his lips into a simulation of a kiss.

"He is drunk." Lucia laughed. "If I had my phone with me I would take a video of this. It could go viral."

"So you got your phone." Guy smiled, "and already you are talking about viral videos. Welcome to the twenty-first century."

"Thank you," Lucia giggled. "I activated mine and my mom's. It feels like the time The Farm Help Society bought us that washing machine. We spent all evening looking at the thing like it was an object from another planet."

Guy chuckled. "Do you want my number?"

"I already have it," Lucia smirked. "It was the first one I saved on the phone. I got it from Earl."

"It is high time. I was surprised to hear from Earl that you have cell phone service at the house." Guy massaged his neck. "Times are changing. It certainly would make it easier on me if Micky and Myrtle had cell service."

"Micky would never use it." Lucia giggled. "He claims these modern gadgets are a conspiracy to kill black people and rot their brains."

"And I tell him that all people use it. He needs to get out more."

"George's shop is far enough for him." Lucia turned back to look at the shop. "It is his city."

The music changed, to *If I Were a Carpenter,* John Holt's version. The man was still dancing in the corner.

"Well, well," Guy stopped, "that's our song. We should dance."

"Our song?" Lucia looked at Guy curiously. "Why?"

"Substitute carpenter for farmer, and we have our song." Guy held out his hand. "Come on, let's have our poor man's version of the ball in the middle of the road. We'll do it to George's orchestra."

Lucia grinned. "Okay."

Guy pulled her close to him until they were standing so close together she had no idea where he started and where she ended.

They danced in the street, moving against each other.

"I have to go away for three weeks," Guy murmured, his breath fanned her face. She could feel his chest rising and falling to the beat of her rapidly beating heart.

"Where?" Lucia whispered.

"Florida. I am going to an Agri Expo. I go every year."

"You do?" Lucia murmured in his shirt she was hardly registering what he was saying. *Did he have to smell so good?*

"I'll be staying with my aunt Sharla and her husband, Tanner."

"I see," Lucia looked up at him.

"I'll be back in time to take you to Kingston."

"Thank you," Lucia nodded. "I'll miss you when you are gone. Like I missed you last weekend."

"I'll miss you too," Guy whispered. They stopped moving to the music. He lowered his head until they were standing forehead to forehead.

"You know what this means right?" Guy asked as he clamped his hand around her waist.

"What?" Lucia's voice trembled.

"It means, that we are exclusive," Guy said seriously. "We made it so right here in the middle of the road near George's corner shop. You are now my girl. No more Ace, he got his ball with you. It's over, whatever you had with him."

"Okay," Lucia said breathlessly, she was finding it difficult to breathe with Guy so near. She trembled, waiting for Guy to kiss her. He was taking his time drawing out the moment until she was almost dizzy with anticipation.

And then he took her mouth and kissed her with sensual intensity. It was as if her heart stopped and then it thundered on faster and wilder than ever before.

Guy stopped the kiss after several minutes. They were both breathing hard. She clung to him as if he were an anchor in a storm.

"Let us get you home," Guy said after several moments.

****

"You are a stupid girl," Aretha said abruptly. When Lucia walked up to the veranda. Lucia almost jumped out of her skin.

She had just had a long drawn out kiss with Guy, and she hadn't wanted him to leave.

The lights were off, so she had no idea that her mother was sitting on the veranda.

"Goodnight mom," Lucia said opening the door and going inside.

Aretha was having none of it. She came behind Lucia and turned on the light.

Forcing Lucia to cover her face, the glare temporarily blinded her.

"You should cover your face in shame." Aretha screeched. "I can't believe I birthed such an imbecile. I just saw you at the gate with Guy, explain that, Lucia."

"There is nothing to explain. He walked me home from church."

"The way the two of you were carrying on, especially you, clinging to him as if he were a lifeline, I am almost certain you learned nothing at church tonight," Aretha growled. "If only I could beat the facts of life into your tough head."

"I know the facts of life, Mom." Lucia cautiously lowered her hand and blinked rapidly. "And I wasn't covering my face in shame. What is there to be ashamed of? I love Guy. I just do, and I don't love Ace. There is nothing that you or anybody can do about it. My heart wants what it wants."

"For goodness sakes!" Aretha bellowed. "Where did you get that nonsense from?"

"Somewhere," Lucia said vaguely. "I am going to bed."

"No, you are not," Aretha growled. "You are going to sit down in this settee," she sat down and pointed to the floral settee across from hers, "and you are going to listen to me."

Lucia sat down and heaved a sigh of discontent. "You can't force me to love Ace."

"I did not say anything about love." Aretha huffed. "I married for love, and my husband tried to kill me."

"After you cheated on him and he found out that you had me for another man," Lucia said patiently.

"I cheated on him because I fell out of love with him." Aretha rebutted. "Which goes to show, that love is fickle."

Lucia sighed and closed her eyes.

"You need a good provider, a man who has a stable and well-respected profession and his own house."

Lucia cracked an eye open. "Can I go to bed now?"

"Yes, why not?" Aretha snarled. "You are your own big woman. It's just that I hate to see you make the same mistakes that I did. My husband was the best-looking man in the district where I grew up. All of the girls were crushing on him. I was envied. I felt like being with him was the best thing I could do.

"I completely skipped over Charles Peters who is now the head of the Peoples Bank, you've seen him on television. That man courted me like there was no tomorrow but I thought that my heart wants what it wants. Keith Gordon was charming and handsome, and I had no mother to tell me that I was making a mistake. My mother had too many of us to worry about my love life. And so I got burned."

"Ah," Lucia rounded her eyes comically. "You are trying to live vicariously through me that's why you are pushing me toward Ace."

"You are heading for a life of misery if you hook up with Guy Wiley. You want me to tell you how this is going to go?"

Lucia folded her arms and looked at her mother mutely. "Is it anything new? You've been telling me how it is going to go since I was seventeen."

Aretha ignored her. "You are so in lust with Guy Wiley you are going to sleep with him and then have his kid, maybe he'll marry you...maybe he won't. Then you'll move to whichever country hole he lives in now. You have no clue where he lives, do you?"

"No," Lucia hissed, "but I am going to find out soon."

"Good lord." Aretha sighed. "When you do find out, you'll see that it is nothing much, but knowing you, you'll convince yourself that it is small but romantic. When he does get you pregnant and move you into the bushes, and you have the child, you'll realize that the hovel can't fit all three of you comfortably. But by this time you'll be dependent on him and the next thing you know you have another kid and then another.

"You'll lose your looks. You'll lose your figure. You will become unattractive to him, and he will move on to some other young pretty girl who looks ten times better."

"Your imagination is overactive, Mom." Lucia grinned. "Besides, you haven't lost your looks or figure."

"Just you wait," Aretha said impatiently. "You will hardly see him after a while, and you will nag him over where he has been and with whom. The more you nag him, the more he'll stay away."

"And then one day you realize that you want to escape but can't because you do not have the bus fare to come to Portland. You'll be so broke, and the children need something to eat, you'll end up begging on the streets."

Lucia rolled her eyes. "That's rubbish."

"Then some married man with a job is nice to you, you sleep with him and has his baby, and then Guy finds out..."

"That's your story." Lucia shook her head. "Stop projecting your story on me."

"Meanwhile," Aretha fanned away her comment, "Ace

marries someone else, a lovely girl, maybe Novalee."

"Novalee?" Lucia giggled. "You can't be serious."

"They live in Kingston. We see them in the society section of the papers when they attend balls together. She goes back to school, does something with her life and looks twenty years younger than you when you are in your early forties."

"Does Charles Peters' wife look twenty years younger than you?"

"Oh yes," Aretha sneered, "She runs that famous gym in Kingston where all the beauty queens go to train."

"Is that the end of your prophesying?" Lucia yawned.

"There might not be a Farm Help Society where Guy Wiley lives in the bushes," Aretha warned. "What are you going to do then? Huh?"

"I will survive." Lucia rubbed her eyes sleepily. "Besides, you'll find me in the bushes, you are better to me than your mother was to you, and when you find me you'll tell me I told you so over and over again, and then you'll take me and the hundreds of children I'll have, and we'll move back in here with you."

Aretha grunted. "I should have known you wouldn't take this seriously."

"And you should stop thinking the worst of Guy and get to know him before you make assumptions about him."

Aretha got up and pulled her nightgown firmly around her. "You should take your own advice and stop mooning over this pretty boy."

Chapter Sixteen

Three weeks without Guy had Lucia feeling slightly bereft. She had never felt his absence so keenly before. They spoke on the phone quite often especially when she was at work, during her lunch break. The cell phone signal at home made for uncomfortable static filled conversations with Aretha giving her the eye when he called.

In the meantime, Ace had stepped up his romantic efforts. He sent flowers to her every day. Her co-workers and some customers were well aware of the great courtship.

Lucia was torn. She liked the attention, it was romantic, but she had already made her choice.

"How do you know if you love somebody?" She asked her brother. They were lazing in the living room after church.

Earl looked at her in consternation. "You are asking me? Why don't you ask one of your girlfriends?"

"Love is not necessary to a relationship, not at the beginning." Aretha entered the hallway still dressed in her church clothes. She looked at Lucia disapprovingly. "Eastern societies have it right. They let the families choose the spouse."

Lucia rolled her eyes and leaned back in the settee. "Seriously mom?"

"Yes seriously." Aretha smiled. "You should allow your elders to choose for you. We are wiser. The Western tradition of dating and finding somebody based on a fickle emotion as love is outright foolishness. Marriage is more than romantic, *swoony* feelings. It is a partnership, a commitment, a merger."

Aretha nodded fiercely. "Would you merge your business with one that's failing or unprofitable, or would you stick with one that's perfectly solvent? "

"Wow, mom. Every day you seem to get more creative at browbeating Lucia about this doctor. And how do you know so many big words about financing?"

Aretha glared at her son. "I read the business section of the paper. As for you Earl Gordon, you are a man and my first born, you should make yourself as attractive as possible for a merger too.

"I'm not only concerned about Lucia. You have just started a good career, and Nate is in college studying to be a doctor. I am satisfied that you are on the right track. If by any stretch of the imagination I thought that you were seeing a country girl from around here who had no ambition I would be on your case as well."

Earl cleared his throat. "I see."

"Are you seeing any of the girls in this area?" Aretha turned narrowed eyes on her son.

"Define see." Earl raised an eyebrow.

"See, as an in talk to, have sex with, considering as a girlfriend."

Earl groaned. "I live in St. Ann, Mom. I am an adult. I

don't want you interfering in my life like you do Lucia's."

"Amen." Lucia murmured.

Aretha swung around to Lucia. "My only girl, who I am determined not to be like me, you won't be escaping that easily. That's why I say, choosing a spouse should be a family decision. You are less likely to make mistakes that way. They have fewer divorces in the countries that still do it that way.

"But I know that you young people don't want to hear that, you are brainwashed into believing the fairytale concept. Oh, you love to be in love. You see stars and hear music and float on cloud nine and think that is enough to build a life together. You have no concept of what is practical. Love cannot put a roof over your head or put clothes on your back or put food on your table."

Earl was the first to snicker. "Goodness, Mom you are militant today."

"No, not militant, struggling to educate children who I am determined will not repeat my foolish mistakes. But I am done for now. I am going with the women's group to visit the hospital and to bring cheer to the sick."

She left the house, and Earl looked at Lucia and grinned. "Your mother is something else."

"Yep." Lucia sighed. "I know, and I think she is making a lot of sense. I understand her fear of history repeating itself, but the truth is she keeps on assuming that in any relationship that I have in the future I will be a dependent. I have my photography skills. I intend to take it to the next level. I am going to be a success with this."

Earl clapped his hands and gave her an approving look. "Independence."

"I wish my mother would at least encourage me instead of throwing Ace in my face every chance she gets."

"Bravo," Earl was nodding vigorously. "So tell me about the new lens and what you are going to be doing with it."

"I can show you." Lucia got up excitedly. "I have loads of pictures to show."

She carried her computer and plunked it on Earl's lap. "I even did a logo."

Earl browsed through her recent catalog. She had spent nearly all of the previous week in Port Antonio town, getting acquainted with the lenses.

"Oh wow!" Earl murmured. "These are pretty."

Lucia went over to see what he was exclaiming about. It was a picture of Novalee in a white church dress and a white straw hat to match. She was smiling; her perfectly white teeth and naturally pink lips could be used for a toothpaste ad.

"The lighting was perfect," Lucia murmured. "No photo editing was needed."

"She's a beautiful girl." Earl nodded. "What is she up to these days? Is she seeing anyone?"

"No, not that I know of." Lucia shook her head; she resisted the urge to tell him about Novalee's potential pregnancy. Novalee had not spoken to her about it since. And she hadn't asked.

Earl stayed on the picture for so long that Lucia chuckled. "There are more of her in there. She insists that I take her picture every chance she gets."

Earl laughed uncomfortably. "I am so obvious."

"She would get the seal of approval from our mother. She is after all the bishop's daughter."

"Yeah," Earl nodded, "but I am nowhere near ready to settle down, Nova is just one pretty girl. There are loads of them in St. Ann who I am interested in."

He quickly skimmed through the rest of the photos and

then nodded. "They are really good. Have you shown them to Guy?"

"No." Lucia shook her head. "Not these but he has seen my older ones. He is not here you know."

"Yeah, he told me." Earl grinned. "He told me to visit every weekend while he was away to make sure that you were not straying."

"He said that?" Lucia gasped.

"Nah," Earl laughed. "Guy doesn't strike me as insecure. He suggested that I keep an eye on things while he is away but you know he didn't have to tell me that."

Lucia's cell phone beeped, and she grabbed it off the center table in anticipation. Guy texted her regularly in the past week. It was easier to text.

But it wasn't Guy it was Ace.

Lunch at my place? My mother wants to meet you. Pick you up in ten minutes.

She sighed. "Ace wants me to have lunch at his place. His mother is here!"

Earl frowned. "Stop stringing Ace along, Lucia. If you are not interested, cut it off."

Lucia nodded. "I will. I try to, but he doesn't listen. He has this quote, "If she's amazing, she won't be easy. If she's easy, she won't be amazing. If she's worth it, you won't give up. If you give up, you're not worthy. ... everybody is going to hurt you; you just gotta find the ones worth suffering for.

"I know it by heart because he has it on a card with a picture of Bob Marley hanging in his car!"

Earl nodded. "Say it again. I like it."

"Argh," Lucia growled. "I shouldn't go, this thing with Ace is not going to work. Meeting his mother is a big deal."

Lucia looked at her brother helplessly. "Help me."

Earl shook his head. "Sorry, Sis. You are going to have to

do this yourself and do it with sensitivity. I haven't broken up with a girl yet, but I know if I invested time and energy in one and I am rejected I would feel raw, trust me."

****

Ace's mother was a female version of him. She was pretty and had the kind of face that made it difficult to guess her age. She looked to be anywhere from her late forties to her sixties. Her hair was dyed jet black, and her makeup was perfectly done. She had on a slash of pink lipstick to match her pink summery dress.

She was pleasant and down to earth and had an easy relationship with her son. She laughed a lot and included Lucia in her stories.

Lucia sat on the back patio with them and found herself relaxing in Celia Jackson's company.

"You know Lucia," Celia said sipping her fruit juice, "I have five sisters. And all of us were named from category five hurricanes except me. I was just a category three."

"Really?" Lucia laughed.

"Yes. Janet was the first. Then there was Carla, Hattie, Beulah, and then Camille. My father was a meteorologist and had a lively sense of humor."

Ace winked at her. "You see our future children would inherit a wonderful trait."

Celia looked at her and smiled. "Ace speaks about you is the way his father Norman speaks about me. In a way, we are similar Lucia.

"I grew up here in the valleys and had just turned twenty when young doctor Ace Jackson came here to work. He was fresh out of university, and the Port Antonio Hospital was his first assignment. I was a nursing aide and admired the young doctor from afar."

Celia chuckled. "It took us six weeks to get married and then we bought this place from old Mr. Hartford. He practically gave it to us."

"I then quit my job, because I wanted to be the lady of the manor. However, I was bored out of my wits with only Myrtle, my housekeeper for company. The place is pretty, but there is nothing much to do around here."

"It didn't help that Myrtle used to mutter that the devil found work for idle hands. So, I took up gardening. It was glorious in the front yard, I tell you."

Lucia nodded. "But you had help didn't you, from Micky Wiley?"

"Yes of course," Celia smiled. "Micky knew his plants very well."

"He still rambles on and on about the good old days." Ace chuckled. "Apparently you had quite a few orange trees."

"Oh yes," Celia's eyes lit up. "I realized they are not here anymore."

"Orange blight disease took them," Ace said, "after you and Dad abandoned the place."

"We had to move on," Celia suddenly looked pensive. "You were born right here in this house." Celia looked around. "So many wonderful memories."

"Which kind of makes it hard to give it up but I am going to sell it," Ace said, "and Dad's practice too."

"Yes, of course," Celia said lightly, but her eyes looked troubled.

She gave Lucia a sad smile. "Nostalgia, I only embrace it for a little while. I am too much of a pragmatist to revel in the good old days. So Lucia what do you do?"

"I work at Wiley Groceries as a cashier, and I am a budding photographer. I want the photography thing to be a full-time career."

"I see." Celia nodded. "You certainly have the vistas around here to take advantage of."

"I do." Lucia nodded, "I like to do weddings as well. As a matter of fact, I am going to do my first wedding in two weeks."

"That's great." Celia smiled wide.

"It will be in Kingston, and she is staying with the Wiley's. Can you imagine that?" Ace huffed, "when she could stay at my apartment."

"The Wiley's?" Celia raised an eyebrow. "Your employers?"

"Yes." Lucia nodded. "My friend Guy told his brother that I needed a place to stay and he kindly offered. I can't turn it down, it was a kind thing to do, and I already said yes."

"Beware of the Wiley men," Celia gave Lucia a long assessing look and then sighed. "They are charmers, seducers, very irresistible men."

"Mother!" Ace bellowed. "That was said with some personal knowledge behind it."

Celia laughed and waved him off. "Oh Ace, I have been around long enough to know one thing, if you love Lucia, you should follow her to Kingston so that she is not tainted with Wiley fever. It burns hot and can consume a girl to the exclusion of all else."

"Can you get me another drink, honey?" Celia asked tapping her empty glass.

"Sure." Ace got up. "Do you want one too, Lucia?"

"Yes, thanks." Lucia nodded.

When he left, Celia gave Lucia a fulsome glare. "What on earth are you doing with my son, Lucia Wray?"

"Huh?" Lucia asked shocked that the pleasant, sweet lady had disappeared and in her place was a fierce looking mother hen.

"My son loves you. You don't love him," Celia whispered.

"You need to end this before it goes further. My boy is like a playful puppy eager to please, and you are just so indifferent."

Lucia sighed. "I want to end it. I love somebody else, but Ace won't take no for an answer. I don't want to hurt him."

"But you will. Rip the band-aid off and stop playing with him," Celia said. "Gentle is not always best."

"I don't have it in me to be that mean to a person," Lucia whispered, "and sometimes I think, what if I am cruel now and one day I collapse, and he is the only doctor around?"

Celia chuckled. "He made an oath to do no harm. He is obligated to help. This somebody else that you love is Guy Wiley, isn't it?"

Celia sniffed, "I saw it in your eyes when you called his name, the Wiley men are lethal."

"But wouldn't that also make Ace lethal?" Lucia asked before she could stop herself.

Celia froze.

She didn't move for a full minute, even when Ace came back with the drinks. "What's wrong, Mom?"

"Nothing," Celia said huskily.

She gave Lucia a warning look. "Nothing at all."

"I was just thinking about something Lucia said." She smiled, but it didn't reach her eyes. "When you come to Kingston Lucia we should have a chat. Maybe we can meet for lunch and have a girls-only time."

Lucia nodded uncertainly. She was sure that Celia was going to quiz her about what she knew. She should have kept her mouth shut.

"And I will be taking some time off too to spend in Kingston," Ace said winking at Lucia. "I can't have the Wiley's upstaging me for your affections. I'll even drop you at the lion's den. I want to know where you are at all times."

"Guy already said he would take me." Lucia sighed. "He

knows where I'll be staying and Walter's wife, Aisha, said she would take me to the wedding and be my assistant if I wanted help and I do. I want to do a video of the event. She sounds very excited about it."

Ace thumped the table in frustration. "So, after the wedding, I'll be there."

"I kind of told Guy that I wanted to see the farm where he works," Lucia said. "I am spending a week up there."

"What?" The veins bulged at the side of Ace's head. "No Lucia. I forbid it!"

Celia was looking between the two of them interestedly.

"Look," Lucia inhaled, "Ace I can't continue to see you, I love Guy."

"No, you don't." Ace growled, "I get the attraction thing. Many women love Guy, and he loves them back. He is a player. He is not the kind of man you plan a future with. He is going to hurt you, and I love you too much to see that happening. I am going to save you from yourself."

"Good heavens, Ace," Celia murmured in the silence, after Ace's outburst.

"You will see sense, Lucia," Ace said gently. "We were meant to be together."

Lucia was at a loss as to what to say next.

Chapter Seventeen

It was a long three weeks for Guy. He delivered a guest lecture at the University of Florida to strawberry growers. Then he joined the Canadian Mensa team for the annual culture quest competition. His team barely won, but it was still a win. And then he spent the rest of his time with his aunt Sharla, his mother's youngest sister.

Sharla and her husband, Tanner, had moved from Canada and were living in Orlando Florida for the past three years.

Their children, Nicholas and Arianna, were away at college. Nicholas had gotten into Harvard and Sharla was so excited about it, she mentioned it every two seconds.

Tanner was a real estate lawyer and Sharla a real estate agent with a luxury firm, but she had quite a bit of downtime on her hands.

Guy was frankly exhausted. His aunt was an energy bunny; he should not have mentioned to her that he was interested in seeing some strawberry farms; she had quite literally dragged him to what seemed like all the strawberry farms in Florida and quite a few in Georgia.

And now on his last day, they were both sitting on the outside patio overlooking the pool. Sharla was cupping a cup of coffee in her hands, and she was looking at him like a proud mother hen.

"We visited twenty-five farms. I now know more about strawberries than I wanted to."

Guy chuckled. "That was all your fault."

"And here I was thinking that the next time I come to Jamaica, I'd be staying at your farm, like the last time." Sharla wrinkled her nose. "I just might change my mind or wait until the scent of strawberry has cleared from my head."

Guy laughed. "You are extra as usual. You loved my farm. You said you wanted to retire there."

"Speaking of extra," Sharla shook her head, "when last have you heard from your cousins?"

"I hear from them all the time." Guy shrugged. "They are okay. Giselle has formed a bond with Pete, Preston's son. They attend the same high school. She is at the Wiley complex on a regular basis, or so Preston tells me.

"Tiana is a nerd like me; we share books all the time, and Elsa wants to model. Jordan thinks it is a bad idea."

Sharla tapped the table. "My mother's intuition is saying all is not right with the girls. I feel as if Brandy is less than adequate as a mother. I wish I had more control over the situation, but that blustery old Toddy Pryce claims that he has things squared away. Whatever does that mean? The idiot."

"He is not so bad." Guy tried to reassure his aunt. "Jordan and I keep in touch regularly. They are okay. Toddy is not the best role model, and Brandy is a bit of a narcissist, but they are growing up to be okay. Like we did."

"I offered to take them a couple of years ago, and the egomaniac said no," Sharla growled. "If that witch Jennifer Riddley Wiley had not taken the lives of my sisters we wouldn't be having this conversation. They would be growing up with the best mother in the world. Monique was the perfect mother to Hannah and me. Such a pity...such a pity..."

"I thought you said you had forgiven Jennifer," Guy murmured.

"I have," Sharla said sheepishly, "it still doesn't stop me from thinking, if only. Sometimes, I think, if only Monique had not gone to the salon that day, if only Hannah had seen Jennifer coming and locked the doors. If only by some miracle Jennifer had shot herself instead of Joseph."

"If only's are counterproductive." Guy sighed.

"I know." Sharla looked at him admiringly, "I know my smart high IQ nephew, member of Mensa I know."

Guy frowned. "I have it from good authority that having a high IQ is nothing compared to having a high EQ."

"Emotional intelligence, the ability to relate to and interact with others, that's what EQ stands for isn't it?" Sharla asked.

"Yes." Guy nodded.

Sharla chuckled. "There is nothing wrong with your EQ. You seem fine to me. Amazingly well adjusted for what you went through when you were only just a boy. All your brothers are amazing, and you've formed normal relationships, thank God."

"Preston has Sheryl, Jordan has Shawn, Saint has Sandrene and Case has that preacher woman, what's her name?"

"Pastor Fifi Daniels," Guy supplied.

"May they be engaged forever," Sharla muttered, "for I do not like her. I pray about them every night. I say Lord intervene in my Case's life. I don't want him marrying that holier than thou monster of a woman."

Guy chuckled. "Come on aunt Sharla, all she did was call you a sinner at the dinner when Case introduced her. She was making a joke. She said all of us were sinners except for Saint. Everybody laughed except you."

"She's too old for him." Sharla frowned, "and I think she is a phony. Nothing more than a holy groupie out to get my nephew because he can sing and he brings revenue to her church."

"Of all your sisters-in-law I am partial to Sandrene. She is genuinely a sweet girl. Of course, I might change my mind if I finally get to meet Lucia. I feel as if I know her already. I have been shopping for her since you formed the Farm Help Society."

"How are things progressing?" Sharla took a sip of her coffee.

"Good." Guy chuckled. "When I left Jamaica, we made it official. She was going to let the doctor down gently and then when I go back. I will tell her all of my secrets."

"And then you'll live happily ever after." Sharla smiled at him, "I like it."

"By the way," Guy said knowing she was going to explode, "Saint is thinking of leaving Sandrene. He says he has fallen out of love with her."

"Nonsense." Sharla widened her eyes, "what kind of rubbish is this?"

"Apparently it happens." Guy shrugged.

"I don't know about that." Sharla frowned. "I need to go to Jamaica to shake some sense into them?"

"I don't know if that will work." Guy shrugged. "I haven't seen Sandrene, but I know that Saint is miserable." He glanced at his watch. "Sharla I don't want to miss my flight. I promised Lucia, I would pick her up from Portland. It will be her first time out of the parish. I want to be there for that."

****

Bags Packed. Check.
All cameras and lenses accounted for. Check.
Anxious mother. Check.

Lucia double-checked her handbag. "I can't believe I am going to Kingston to work. This is surreal."

"Don't do anything stupid." Aretha wrinkled her brow. "Why do you have to go for two weeks?"

"Because I want to see other places, experience other adventures." Lucia zipped up the last bag and slung her camera around her neck. "It will be fun."

"What about food?" Aretha asked. "You have money for food and money to get home in case Guy's vehicle breaks down on the road?"

Lucia nodded. "Yes, I do, Mom. Stop worrying."

"Okay." Aretha sighed. "I guess since Guy's rich relatives are putting you up you won't be in a ghetto, will you?"

"No," Lucia said uncertainly, "I have no idea where it is."

Aretha nodded. "Call me."

"I will." Lucia nodded. She carried her bags to the small veranda and waited for Guy to arrive. As usual, he was on time; he pulled up in his newish green pick up.

"At least this one is slightly better than the other one." Aretha sniffed.

"Be nice," Lucia whispered.

Guy got out of the vehicle looking yummy as usual. He was wearing jeans and a white polo shirt. His jet-black curly hair was falling over his broad forehead in sexy disarray."

Lucia looked at her mother and grinned. "There is such a thing as a perfect guy."

"A perfect looking guy." Aretha sniffed. "Looks, however,

can fade. Just remember the seven children you'll have in the country with no money for support while he is out gallivanting with newer, fresher women."

Lucia laughed out loud.

Guy kept the greetings short. Aretha glared at him the whole time he was putting Lucia's bags in the truck.

"What did I do to her?" Guy asked when they drove off.

"She is just a concerned mother." Lucia giggled. "She has this theory that I am going to shack up with you and have loads of kids and live on the farm where you work."

Guy grinned. "Shack up, no. No way. Marriage is what I want. And not a load of children, I was thinking more of about four."

Lucia widened her eyes. "Four?"

Guy nodded. "A nice even number."

"I was thinking one," Lucia murmured, "just one."

"I can live with that." Guy smiled at her and squeezed her hand. "So how did it go with Ace?"

Lucia's eyes clouded over. He said that I don't know what I want and that he is going to save me from making a mistake.

"Fighting talk," Guy murmured. "I didn't expect that."

"Let's talk about something else," Lucia said, "like your visit to Florida. What was it like?"

"It was good." Guy smiled, "I visited a lot of farms with my aunt."

He glanced at her. "If Ace is going to be a problem, I can talk to him, set him right. You know what, I think I should do that."

"You may get the chance sooner than you think," Lucia sighed. "He said something about coming to Kingston."

Guy nodded. "Well, okay then. I'll be around. You still up for coming to stay with me at the farm."

"Sure. Yes!" Lucia beamed. "I can't believe this. I'll finally know where you go when you leave Portland."

Guy nodded. "It is time. I want to be completely open and upfront with you going forward. I have a couple of things to tell you too."

Lucia looked at him and frowned. "Bad things?"

"No," Guy grinned, "I don't think it is. I'll have to build some courage to tell you though."

"Just tell me," Lucia said.

They were driving through Buff Bay. The bustling seaside town was a mish-mash of rustic buildings and more modern architecture all beside a sea wall. The day was slightly overcast, the lighting perfect.

"I will." Guy watched her as she looked around interestedly. She was distracted from their conversation and was absently caressing the camera around her neck.

"Want us to stop so that you can take pictures?" He asked smiling.

"Yes please!" Lucia nodded. "Can we go back just a bit so that I can get the seawall and the town in the distance?"

"Sure," Guy said, he turned into a parking lot and headed back to the outskirts of the town.

Lucia looked at him apologetically, "I am so sorry about this."

"It is okay," Guy looked at his watch. "Take your time. It is just three o'clock. We have plenty of daylight time to indulge you."

"Cool." Lucia nodded. "Please pose right there."

She pointed to the wall.

"Me?" Guy sighed. "You are going to have to do the same. You know that right?"

Lucia grinned. "I am not usually before the camera."

"And we are going to have to do some with the two of us." Guy insisted. "I am pretty sure you have loads of shots of me."

"You know about that?" Lucia widened her eyes. "You know that I secretly take pictures of you?"

Guy chuckled. "Earl may have made it slip in a conversation or two."

"My big mouth brother." Lucia hissed.

"Your big mouth brother wanted to give me hope that you are interested in me." Guy walked around to her side of the vehicle until they were standing directly in front of each other. Close enough so that their noses were touching.

"You are tall you know that?" Guy grinned. "Perfect height for me."

"You are a little taller than me." Lucia smiled. "And I am in wedge heels."

"You feel that?" Guy whispered.

"What?" Lucia whispered.

"My heartbeat," Guy said before he kissed her.

****

The two and a half hour journey from Port Antonio to Kingston took them six hours. They stopped everywhere for Lucia to indulge herself in taking pictures and at a restaurant to eat.

By the time Guy rolled into the Wiley Complex, it was dark out.

Lucia looked out of the window with a dazed air. "Which hotel is this?"

"The Wiley Hotel." Guy chuckled. "Actually it is several townhouses and not a hotel."

"Oh my," Lucia murmured. "When your brother said a house beside his, I was picturing something different."

Guy stopped in front of his townhouse. Hoping that Lucia wouldn't comment on his familiarity with the place. He wasn't ready to confess yet. He didn't know what he was waiting for. She had obviously chosen him over Ace Jackson. Him. Guy the farmer. Mission accomplished. What was he waiting on?

The right time perhaps.

He had it all planned out in his head, Lucia would visit him at the farm, he would tell her he didn't just work there and that it was his.

His housekeeper, Catherine was already briefed and excited to meet her. He would show her around.

Then he would pop the question. If she said yes, then he would confess that he was also the Farm Help Society and that it was a big elaborate ruse to help out her and her family anonymously.

"Come on," Guy got out of the vehicle and knocked on the front door.

Aisha was already briefed that she would be the welcoming party of one.

And Aisha was up for it. She pulled the door opened and gave Guy a broad smile,

"Hi, Guy." She almost spoiled it with a conspiratorial wink. "What took you so long? You left out at three."

"I had to indulge the photographer," Guy murmured and then frowned at her. "Tone down the friendliness to me."

"Okay," Aisha chuckled, "I have been practicing, but fair warning. Sheryl and Shawn are here in the living room. Walter is planning to stop by, and I heard Jordan and Preston are going to do the same."

Guy groaned. "Seriously?"

"Seriously!" Aisha shook her head. "Who can blame them, we have all been dying to meet her especially when Walter reported that she looks like an exquisite Barbie doll and he wasn't sure that you were going to win versus the doctor. Apparently, he had his hand all over her at the ball."

"But she chose me," Guy whispered. "I didn't take her to any fancy balls or told her that I had two cents to rub together. And you and the rest of my family are going to play it cool. Do not give me away. I will do the big reveal in my own time."

Aisha chuckled and looked past him to Lucia sitting in the van. "I will play along; I can't vouch for Shawn or Sheryl though. You know Shawn needs a filter."

"Meddling women," Guy muttered.

"I heard that," Shawn tiptoed up to the door. "I can't pretend that you are a stranger Guy. Nothing is wrong if I tell her that we grew up together."

Guy sighed. "Just keep your sharing to a minimum."

Guy went to the van for Lucia; she looked at him suddenly shy and uncertain. "Is she nice?"

"Very nice," Guy whispered.

"Welcome Lucia," Aisha gushed moving from the door and hugged Lucia.

Lucia visibly relaxed.

"I must apologize for the intrusion," Aisha said smiling, "but my sisters-in-law decided to stop by for a while."

"Are you hungry, want something to drink?"

She ushered Lucia into the house and left Guy outside to get the bags.

Chapter Eighteen

Lucia could barely take it all in at once. The townhouse was gorgeous; Aisha and her sisters-in-law were all very beautiful women. Shawn was obviously outgoing, Sheryl was more reserved but warm, and Aisha was helpful and friendly. Lucia instantly found herself feeling relaxed in their company. They were lovely people.

Guy carried in her bags upstairs and then sat and chatted with them for a while. Aisha showed her around. The kitchen was well stocked with enough food to feed an army. Her mother's fretting about her not having food was now laughable in the face of such abundance.

From the conversation, Lucia learned that Shawn was the one who designed and decorated the place. She was an engineer.

An honest to goodness engineer. Lucia's head had not stopped spinning from that revelation.

And then she heard that Sheryl was head of sales at Wiley

Corp.

They both had children and were working mothers.

Aisha was a math teacher, who had turned down a job offer at a bank because she loved school holidays.

They were all accomplished women who could stand on their two feet if they wanted to. Her mother should meet them.

"This family could do well with a professional photographer." Shawn winked at Guy. "Hint hint."

Guy growled. "Zip it, Shawn Marie."

Shawn laughed and threw a cushion at him. "I won't zip it, brat."

They were obviously close. Why had she thought that Guy was estranged from his siblings or that they were distant?

Shawn treated him like a much-loved brother.

Shawn must have seen the question in her eyes when she said, "Guy and I grew up together."

"That's right," Sheryl piped in.

"You too." Lucia widened her eyes. "You grew up with Guy too?"

"Oh yes." Sheryl nodded. "I even remember going with Guy to the valleys where you are from. Is it still as beautiful?"

"Yes, it is." Lucia nodded, "I have loads of pictures."

"Have any of Micky and Myrtle?" Shawn asked, "I haven't had the time to visit him in a long time. Micky and I go way back you know. We entered the blue Marlin boating tournament together one year."

"Really? Just the two of you?" Lucia was amazed. "Shawn looks like a petite girly girl," Lucia said out loud.

And that was met with laughter.

"I went to high school as a boy for a year," Shawn giggled, "but that is another story."

"You also entered the tournament as a boy," Guy chuckled.

"Don't leave out that part."

"Yup," Shawn grinned, "and don't forget that Micky was drunk as a skunk when we entered the tournament and Preston and Jordan were concerned that we would capsize at sea but I knew Micky had it in him and I was up for the adventure with my partner."

Lucia chuckled. "I have pictures of Micky, he likes posing for me and Myrtle too, but only when she is in her Sunday best."

"I would eat some of Myrtle's stewed chicken with green bananas and callaloo right now," Aisha said licking her lips. "I would take a trip to the valleys just to eat and come back."

Lucia laughed. "She is the best cook."

"I second that, but above all else, Myrtle's sweet potato puddings are unparalleled in taste and texture," Sheryl said, "I can just taste it right now. "

"I have some in the car." Guy piped in. "She sent one for each family."

Sheryl got up. "Show me the way, Guy Wiley. Very impertinent of you to save that piece of information till now."

Guy and Sheryl headed to the van.

"I am going to secure mine," Shawn said heading behind them. "Sheryl sounded too into them puddings."

Aisha chuckled. "I didn't grow up with Guy, like Sheryl and Shawn but I have known Guy for many years."

"Are you serious? And he never got with any of you? You are all so beautiful." Lucia exclaimed.

"What a precious girl." Shawn was heading into the door when she said that. She came over to where Lucia was sitting and hugged her. "You are a keeper."

"Shawn," Guy groaned.

"She is." Shawn laughed and then said to Lucia earnestly. "The truth is I could have never gotten into it with Guy.

Despite how pretty he is, I have only ever had brotherly feelings toward him."

"And there was the fact that Jordan would kill us if we looked at Shawn too hard," Guy muttered. "Jordan had Shawn earmarked for him since they were tots. Our mothers were best friends and ran a hairdressing parlor from our house."

"Oh wow," Lucia nodded, "so you are Jordan's wife?"

"Oh yes," Shawn laughed, "though he didn't ask me to marry him. You should hear our story."

In the middle of Shawn telling their story, Jordan came over.

"Just came to meet Lucia." He shook her hand. "Nice to meet you. My brother talks about you so much I had to at least meet you face to face. I have a sleeping toddler at home."

He patted the baby monitor on his hip. "I had to make sure that she was out."

Lucia had no sooner smiled and greeted him when a boy that looked very much like Jordan followed him; he had a toddler on his hip.

"Hello Lucia," the boy greeted. "I am Pete this is my sister, Petra."

Lucia smiled. "Lovely to meet you. You look so much like your father."

She looked between him and Jordan. "It's amazing the similarity."

Pete chuckled. "Actually I do look like my father. It's just that my father is not uncle Jordan. My father is Preston."

"That would be me," Preston said behind them. "God, it is crowded in here."

And Lucia got to meet Preston and then Walter and Saint. All the brothers except for Case.

And she got a crash course in who was married to who and whose children was whose.

And she made a mental note that Guy was not the odd man out. He was close to his family. His brothers and their wives.

She sat there and observed them as the conversation ebbed and flowed around her.

This was a tight-knit family, and all the brothers were without a doubt uniquely handsome. Lucia was at a loss as to where to look. Preston and Jordan were classically handsome and shared quite similar features. She was hard pressed not to think they were twins.

Saint had green eyes and looked like a picture in one of her Sunday School books of an angel. Then there was Walter, the hunk. She was sure he was the envy of all the men in the gym.

She could see that he was ripped in a suit but dressed casually he was something else. Her eyes skittered from face to face as she familiarized herself with the Wiley clan.

"It gets overwhelming seeing them in one place at first," Aisha whispered to her. "You'll get used to it."

"Are you sure?" Lucia whispered back. "This is some gene pool."

"Trust me," Aisha laughed. "And now it is time to get them out of your hair."

"Okay, everyone Lucia needs to acclimatize herself to her new environment and to unwind, her first gig is tomorrow. We want her rested."

"Have fun, Lucia. I hope you do a fantastic job," Preston said on his way out.

"I want to see some of your pictures of Portland before you leave," Sheryl said. "My department is responsible for the calendars this year, and I have been toying with the idea of featuring Portland."

"Oh my that would be lovely," Lucia nodded. "Sure."

"We are leaving to go back to the job site in two days," Shawn said, "Come and check me for stories about Guy. I have loads of them."

"I will." Lucia nodded. "Definitely."

"Is there any way I can stop this?" Guy groaned. "Anyway at all."

"Hell no," Shawn chuckled. "She needs to know what she is getting herself into. Did you know he is a certified genius, Lucia? As in, IQ above the charts, Mensa certified and all?"

Lucia shook her head. "No, I didn't know that."

"He has even gotten some temperate zone plants to grow here in tropics and won awards for it but best of all, I have baby and teenage pictures. There was a time when Jordan and I were into photography as well. We'll have a good time."

They all left her, Guy and Aisha.

"Oh my goodness," she turned to them, "Preston Wiley is my bosses, bosses, boss. His wife wants to see my pictures for the Wiley calendar, and Shawn has pictures of Guy when he was a baby!"

Aisha chuckled and headed to the door. "I'll be over in the morning to discuss my assistant duties and get directions to the venue. Tomorrow I am all yours."

"Thank you so much," Lucia said. "You are so kind. You all are so kind."

"Think nothing of it. I will do anything within reason for you. Guy is my friend and any friend of Guy's is my friend too."

She smiled and let herself out.

"I am having trouble taking in all this," Lucia whispered she plopped herself in the settee beside Guy. "I am truly overwhelmed right now."

Guy draped his hand across her shoulders, and they sat in

companionable silence for a while.

"So they all live here?" Lucia asked slowly.

"Yep. The complex is called The Wileys."

"So all the Wiley brothers have a house in this complex?" Lucia worried her teeth over her lip.

"That's right." Guy nodded.

"So whose house is this?" Lucia asked looking around.

"Mine," Guy said simply. "I asked Walter to invite you here."

Lucia looked at him. Guy could see the many questions in her eyes.

"So what's up with Suzy?" She finally asked.

"Suzy, my beloved Suzy, bought her off somebody who desperately needed the money. She had character."

Guy looked at her cautiously; she seemed to be taking it well.

"And the farm in the hills? Is it real?"

"Yes, it is." Guy sighed. "It is mine. I was going to make a big production out of telling you, but then my relatives just had to come over tonight."

Lucia chuckled. "They are nice people."

"Lovely." Guy sighed. "I hope this doesn't change anything for us and that you don't like me any less."

"Love." Lucia smiled, "and it does change things. I liked the idea of the two of us working together to drag ourselves out of poverty. I would make a killing with my photography business, and you would reap a ton of mangos from your trees, and then we'd build a board cottage and then add on to it later."

Guy chuckled. "A board cottage?"

"Yes," Lucia said sleepily. "But now I see how ridiculous those dreams are—you are a rich genius."

"I am who I always was," Guy whispered.

But he was talking to a sleeping Lucia. She was out like a light in no time.

Guy marveled that she fell asleep so quickly and without warning.

"I love you too." Guy kissed her on her forehead. "Now and forever."

She mumbled something unintelligible in her sleep. He took her upstairs to the guest room, laying her on the bed and then watched as she curled up in a ball, oblivious to where she was.

The passageway light was motion activated if she woke up in the middle of the night she would be okay. He went to his room and stared up at the ceiling. He was glad she found out. It made things much easier. Surely nothing stood between him and his happily ever after with Lucia now.

He fell asleep with a smile on his face.

Chapter Nineteen

Lucia woke up in a huge bed that smelled faintly of jasmine. It took her a while to get her bearings and when she did it all came rushing back to her. This was Guy's house. He was close to his family. He must have carried her upstairs.

Where was he?

And how was she going to digest this new and unfamiliar Guy? The image in her head of him was completely shattered. All of this took some digesting but now was not the time to do it. She had to reach the venue by nine. It was six-thirty; she had two and a half hours to get her game face on and to do what she came to Kingston to do.

She was filled with nerves when she went downstairs but was pleasantly surprised to see that Guy was already up. Sitting around the kitchen island and looking at a computer.

"Good morning," Guy greeted her, "you look rested."

"Yes," Lucia smiled shyly. "There is something about this place. In the Aesop fable of the country mouse and the town mouse, do you know if the country mouse slept like a log when he came to the town?"

Guy chuckled. "I can't remember them sleeping over. I remember the town mouse visiting his cousin in the country and was given a simple breakfast. Town mouse scoffed at it because of its simplicity. When it was time to return the favor the town mouse laid out a spread, the remnants of a feast, no less. But after eating, two dogs entered the scene and the mouse had to run for their lives. And the country mouse said, better a simple meal with peace than a feast with fear.

"That said, do you want some breakfast? I can rustle up something simple."

"No thanks," Lucia chuckled, "I couldn't eat in peace even if this weren't the city. It is too early, and I am feeling a little nervous."

"Have you seen my camera case?"

"I took it up to your room," Guy said.

"I have my picture schedule in there," Lucia said. "I hope I didn't leave it. If I need Aisha what do I do?"

"Call her," Guy pointed at the phone, "or go outside and yell for her name. She is just next door."

Lucia nodded. "I think I'll be civilized. I don't want your brothers thinking that I am not."

Guy chuckled. "Then the phone it is."

The nervousness didn't leave her even when she went to the guesthouse in the hills where the wedding took place; the bride was pleasant and friendly when she went to take pre-wedding pictures.

It was a small wedding; the couple had fifty guests. To her horror, one of the guests was Celia Jackson, Ace's mother.

"That lady keeps staring at you with her mouth opened," Aisha came to her during the reception.

"That's Ace's mom," Lucia whispered. "How is it going for you?"

"Good." Aisha nodded. "I love weddings. This does not feel like work. Is Ace, the doctor who was competing for your affections?"

"Yes." Lucia nodded. "That's the one."

"His mother is coming over," Aisha murmured. "I am going to see if I can get some more footage over there."

Lucia nodded. "I can use something for the outtakes. I think we are done here."

"I didn't know this was the wedding you were going to do," Celia came over to Lucia and smiled, it didn't reach her eyes.

"It is," Lucia replied awkwardly.

"Well," Celia smiled, "Candice is my goddaughter. Her mother and I go way back."

Lucia nodded. "That's nice."

"Ever since my lunch with you and Ace, I have been anxious for us to talk. Is tomorrow okay with you?"

Lucia looked down at her camera and adjusted the ISO knob unnecessarily.

"Listen, Celia, I spoke out of turn at lunch, I didn't know what I was talking about. There is no need for you and me to have a conversation about it."

"There is every need," Celia said huffily. "In the thirty-two years since Ace was born, I have never had such a shock. Such a ludicrous assertion made about my child."

"Then I am sorry I brought it up," Lucia said simply, "Ace will never hear it from me. I won't say a word."

"That's good," Celia sniffed, "but where on earth did you come up with such a ludicrous idea?"

"I spoke out of turn." Lucia felt embarrassed. There was no way she would be dragging Guy's name into it, so she said instead. "He does have a Wiley look about him. His eyes..."

"Coincidence!" Celia hissed. "Pure unadulterated coincidence! Ace Junior is Ace Senior's child. Do you hear me? It's not up for debate or speculation, and I implore you not to breathe a word of that ridiculous observation to anyone. People will see what they want to see when they start looking."

Lucia nodded. "I hear you."

"A child's paternity is serious and not a lottery. I am not a gambling woman especially with my children's paternity and you implying otherwise was insulting." Celia hissed. "You intimated that I had an affair with Micky Wiley."

"I never said who..." Lucia frowned. "I just said he was a Wiley too."

"Doesn't matter," Celia fanned her off, "mind your own business next time. You got that?"

Lucia nodded rapidly. She felt soundly chastised, but she did not believe a word of Celia's bluster.

"That's basically what I wanted to tell you at lunch, and I hope we never have to see each other again."

Celia walked off before Lucia could formulate another apology.

****

The pictures came out well, and the added video footage was well done. She spent the next day editing and adding music to the images.

Guy had gone to his farm to return for her the next day. Aisha spent the day with her.

She watched reruns of Golden Girls and chuckled to herself. Sometimes she told Lucia stories about her and Walter and how they met in college and meeting him up again. Aisha even made lunch, and they ate together.

"These spiralized vegetables taste so good." Lucia couldn't stop exclaiming about them. "I could eat this every day."

Aisha nodded. "I do. It's easy and so simple to prepare."

They chit-chatted for the day and then Aisha left to get ready for a party she and Walter were throwing on their patio.

According to Aisha, Walter was happiest when he was arranging a party. One of their church sister's was going away to live in Switzerland, and of course, Walter had to throw a party.

Aisha invited Lucia, but she wanted to finish up what she was doing.

Sheryl stopped by after work just when she was almost done.

"That was a gorgeous wedding," Sheryl said looking over the pictures. "You captured the moments perfectly, very well done, Lucia."

"Thank you," Lucia beamed. She was happy that someone else said out loud what she was thinking. The outcome had surpassed her expectations and then some. Walter's lenses had been top of the line.

"Let me see your other pictures," Sheryl said.

Lucia showed her a collage of pictures and Sheryl nodded approvingly. She paused for a while at a picture of some children playing by the Blue Lagoon.

"This should be called nostalgia. This could be me, Shawn, Jordan, and Preston."

Lucia looked over her shoulder. "You guys used to hang there."

"A lot." Sheryl nodded.

"So you and Preston were together for a long, long time," Lucia widened her eyes, "and still going strong, obviously."

"Our story is a convoluted one." Sheryl smiled ruefully,

"we weren't together for a couple of years, but found each other again. Love always wins."

Lucia nodded. "So I have heard."

Sheryl got up. "I expect we'll be family soon, but that is not why I am going to commission you to do our calendars. I need twelve pictures of Portland, send me fifty of your best. I'll have the office staff vote on which ones to put on the calendar."

"Oh my goodness, thank you!" Lucia squealed.

"We'll talk compensation a next time." Sheryl smiled at her. "Deadline is the end of August."

Lucia nodded.

She ended up dancing around the living room by herself and then her phone rang.

She answered without looking at the phone display.

It was Ace.

"How was it?" Ace asked after they said their hellos.

"Great! I stayed up all day and edited the pictures and the videos. They didn't expect video, but I am giving it to them." Lucia gushed. She was in such a good mood she didn't notice that Ace didn't sound much like himself.

"Has Novalee called you?" Ace asked.

"No." Lucia settled down in the settee and then chuckled. "But why would she? Novalee is never really happy with my successes; she wouldn't care about the outcome."

"I am glad you realized that she is not a loyal friend," Ace said. "I wouldn't call her a friend at all."

"Why would you say that?" Lucia asked.

"She fainted at church yesterday." Ace sighed. "The bishop stopped the service and called for a doctor. That's when Novalee confessed that she is pregnant."

"She is?" Lucia gasped, "I thought it was a false alarm or something she never mentioned that she got a positive result."

"Well, she is." Ace sighed. "The bishop is livid, as can be expected, and Novalee won't say who the father is."

Lucia's heart started racing, and she clutched the phone nervously. She had the premonition that bad news was about to come.

"Lucia," Ace said softly, "she told me who it was, she wanted me to let you know because she couldn't face you."

"No, stop it." Lucia croaked. "She is a liar."

"She said its Guy's child." Ace continued.

"No," Lucia was shaking her head as if he could see her. "No, she is lying. I asked Guy, and he said no."

"Calm down," Ace said soothingly. "Do you want me to come and get you?"

"No." Lucia bellowed, tears were streaming down her face unchecked. She swiped them away angrily. "I am going to call Guy, and he is going to say no."

"And will that reassure you?" Ace asked exasperatedly, "Novalee is pregnant. He needs to focus on his pregnant lover at the moment before anybody else. This baby needs to come first. You know what it feels like when your father ignored you. Stop making excuses for Guy and let him meet up to his responsibilities."

"He wouldn't deny his own child." Lucia said hoarsely, "Guy is not like my father."

"He is worse." Ace hissed, "Novalee said he knew she might be pregnant and they continued to have sex."

"Shut up!" Lucia turned off the phone and covered her head with the sofa cushion. She could hear her heart throbbing in her head.

This was not happening, this was a nightmare, and she was about to wake up at any moment.

She waited and waited for the dream to end, but it didn't.

She heard the ticking of the clock on the mantelpiece. She listened to the faint sound of music. Walter's party.

She held herself very still while the song played, *time goes on, people touch and then they're gone...*

How apt. Lucia roused herself out of her stupor. She didn't know how long she laid curled up in a fetal-like position before she dialed Guy's number.

"Hey," Guy answered happily. "You were on my mind; I was just about to call you."

"Guy," Lucia asked hoarsely, "do you have any secrets at all that you need to tell me. Remember you were starting to tell me something when we were at Buff Bay, and I asked if it was bad?"

"As a matter of fact," Guy paused, "Lucia, I was going to tell you when I come by to pick you up tomorrow."

"You were?" Lucia's heart and head started throbbing in tandem. So this has nothing to do with you being a genius or that you are rich and own a farm or you are the Wiley behind the Wiley produce in the supermarket?"

"Well no," Guy sighed, "I think we shouldn't have any secrets between us, I should have said something from our first kiss, but I didn't know how to tell you. I kept it in for so long and..."

"This is too much. I can't stay here tonight." Lucia choked, her voice tear clogged. "I can't believe this."

"Lucia, what's going on?"

"You and your secrets!" Lucia growled. "You are not honest with me; you have too many secrets, you hide stuff from me. I thought you were different."

"Come on Lucia, where is all of this coming from?" Guy was puzzled. "I was always going to tell you everything. I just never found the right time. Your reaction is crazy; you know that?"

"No, it is not," Lucia growled. "You know Guy, I am going to say this now. I don't want to see or speak with you ever again."

"What?" Guy exploded over the phone. "Why?"

"It is over. Goodbye. Have a nice life." Lucia hung up the phone and burst into tears.

She called Ace.

"Can you come and get me? I want to get out of here."

"Sure, I am in Kingston," Ace said, "I expected this. Where are you?"

"I have no clue," Lucia sobbed. "It's called The Wiley's in a fancy neighborhood."

"The Wiley's," Ace said slowly, "I know where that is. My brother Trey lives near there. I'll be there for you, Lucia."

Chapter Twenty

"**S**he left? Just like that?" Preston and Jordan asked the question almost at the same time.

"Women," Saint muttered, "I think something is wrong with them."

"Certain women," Shawn said sternly. "Some of us are rational."

Guy paced in front of his family running his hand through his curls until his head looked wild.

"Nobody saw her? Talked to her?"

"I spent the whole day with her," Aisha said, "when I left her she was fine."

"When I left her she was happy too." Sheryl offered. "I told her I was going to use her for next year's calendar and she was delighted."

"I saw her." Pete offered, "I was coming from the pool when I saw her getting into a black Pajero. The man came out and got her bags. She was crying."

"For goodness sakes!" Guy muttered. "Black Pajero that's Ace Jackson."

"What did you say to make her cry?" Jordan asked.

"She asked me if I had any secrets. I said yes as a matter of fact I do and then I said I wanted to tell her tomorrow and she spazzed out and said she doesn't want to see me again etcetera, etcetera."

"I knew the Farm Help Society nonsense would have gotten you in trouble," Preston said. "She must have heard that you were behind it and had the opposite reaction to what you thought she would have."

"But that wasn't exactly tragic news. Why would she call the competition? To save her from big bad patient Guy who has financed her and her whole family for the past five years!" Walter said heatedly. "Who does that?"

"Go after her and straighten it out," Jordan said.

"She says she doesn't want to see or speak with me ever again." Guy finally stopped pacing and sat down on the settee. He was genuinely confused. "I don't want her to think that she is obligated to be with me either. I never wanted that. If it freaks her out that I was the charity behind it all, I will have to let her go."

"Ungrateful heifer!" Shawn muttered.

"Let's not jump to conclusions." Jordan looked at Shawn warningly. "She could still be Mrs. Guy Wiley when all of this is straightened out, and you don't want to be the one who called Guy's future wife names."

Shawn snorted inelegantly. "You are right, I am sorry. I don't understand why the Wiley brothers' women are filled with so much drama."

"Said the chief drama queen of us all," Sheryl murmured.

"I say forget her, count your losses," Saint offered. "Yes, you helped her and her family, yes she is pretty to look at and seemed okay, but they all start out that way. One day four years down the road you'll fall out of love with her and then comes the divorce. Better to know now."

"Don't listen to Saint." Sheryl sat beside Guy and put her hand around his shoulders, "He is bitter right now, and his wife does seem to be going through a personality crisis."

"I'd say," Shawn grunted, "I called to her the other morning, and she blanked me. Looked right through me. Then when I walked up to her, she gave me the fakest smile and said hi in a high-pitched fake kind of way that had me wanting to punch her. I have never wanted to punch Sandrene before."

Saint nodded. "Me neither."

"But we digress," Jordan said looking at Guy. "Do you love her, Guy?"

"Yes." Guy nodded. "I do."

"Then fight for her." Jordan shrugged. "Get her back, straighten out whatever it is that needs to be straightened out. Grovel if you have to."

****

Fighting for Lucia was easier said than done. She wasn't answering her phone. He showed up at her house the next day and was met by Aretha who seemed very irate with him.

"You are a destroyer of women, Guy Wiley." Aretha huffed. "I have never seen Lucia so broken up before. I hope she can recover. You are scum."

"What did I do?" Guy asked wearily. He was existing on no food or sleep. He was just weary and confused.

"You should ask Novalee what you did, you pig." Aretha slammed the door in his face.

He drove to the supermarket with one thought in mind; he needed to get to the bottom of this madness.

When Novalee saw him, she squealed and hugged him like he was some long lost friend. She was so openly friendly and clingy he was further thrown off guard.

"Let's talk outside by your car," Novalee said, loud enough for the other cashiers to hear. "I'll meet you there; I am just going to have somebody cover for me."

Guy went outside and leaned on his vehicle. Impatiently waiting for Novalee to enlighten him about what was going on.

He didn't have long to wait; she came barreling out of the supermarket in excitement. "You are driving a Range!"

"Huh?" Guy looked at her, not realizing what she was saying until it sunk in. The air-headed girl was excited about his car.

"Yes," he said impatiently. "Novalee, what is wrong with Lucia? Why am I suddenly the last person on earth she wants to see? Things were going great."

"I don't know," Novalee was walking around his car excitedly. "She gave me a note for you, yesterday. She figured you would show up here."

Novalee took it out of her pants pockets and then clapped her hands in glee. "Guy can I get a drive, I mean can you drop me home? It's near the end of my shift."

Guy took the note and sighed. "I need some shut-eye. Yes, I guess, if you want a ride home, I can wait."

"Thank you!" Novalee ran up to him and kissed him on the cheek. "You are awesome."

He opened the letter while Novalee ran inside. It was typewritten.

Dear Guy,

I need some space away from you to think things through. If you love me any at all, you will stay away for a while. I need to clear my head.

Guy crumpled the note in frustration.

He didn't even crack a smile when Novalee came into the car like a happy puppy.

"Oh goodness, these seats are real leather aren't they and it adjusts to your butt."

Guy grunted. He wasn't in the mood to talk about his car.

"I knew you were the Farm Help Society," Novalee said grinning at him. "I just knew it. You are not poor, are you? Did you know that Lucia does not appreciate the Jimmy Choo shoes you keep giving her?"

"My finances are none of your business," Guy growled at Novalee. He was feeling hard done by and not very much in the need for conversation. Who knew that an act of anonymous kindness would have blown up in his face this badly?

He turned on the radio instead. Novalee didn't seem to mind. She was twisting and turning in the seat like she had ants in her clothes. She wound down the window and waved to everybody they passed.

Guy thought something was seriously wrong with how manically happy she was acting.

He dropped her home, and the bishop came out of the house.

"May I talk with you young man?"

Goodness, did everybody know that he was the Farm Help Society and was having a major breakdown about it?

He would think that the bishop of all the people would understand that he just saw a family in need and decided to help.

"Daddy leave him alone," Novalee hissed at her father. "He is not the one."

"I do not like deception young man, and I can't abide by this sort of thing happening, and I stand by and not say anything. Are you going to marry her?"

"I wanted to." Guy frowned, "but she is avoiding me. What else can I do?"

"Oh," the bishop glared at Novalee and then turned to him and smiled. "I will talk some sense into her. I wish things were not handled in this way, you understand."

"I understand, but there was a need and I..." Guy sighed, "I should have been upfront about it."

"That's right, there is a process, but I will blame this on youthful exuberance." The bishop nodded conclusively. "Say no more I will make sure that things are sorted. You love her don't you?"

"Yes!" Guy almost shouted in relief, "I didn't know that doing things secretly would have such an unexpected effect. Goodness, if I had known, I would have shouted it out to the neighborhood."

"No need to get so carried away," the bishop looked alarmed, "we don't want the whole neighborhood to know. The family would like to pretend that this went on the normal way but we can't wait too long before it becomes obvious and everybody starts talking about it. I have a reputation to maintain."

Guy nodded. He was a bit slow in connecting the dots with how the neighborhood knowing that he was the Farm Help Society would affect the bishop's reputation. Was he afraid that people would say that the church should have helped instead?

"Thank you Bishop Rochester, you are a good man," he said wearily. "I have been up since last night after I heard. I am going to get some shuteye and something to eat."

The bishop beamed. "You do that. We will talk some more, have some concrete plans going forward. We will do so soon."

Guy tooted and drove off.

Chapter Twenty-One

"**I** heard that he is going to marry Novalee soon," Aretha said while she was folding clothes. "Dr. Jackson said that the bishop told him this himself."

Lucia couldn't believe it. She was sitting in the settee half comatose. She had roused herself to send off the pictures and videos to her client and was staring at the check without much interest.

"Novalee wanted to know if she could come over and discuss wedding dressed with you?"

"Tell her to rot in hell," Lucia growled.

"Lucia snap out of it, Guy Wiley showed you his true colors. He wasn't genuine. He wasn't honest. He was rotten to the core. Pursuing you while having sex with your friend."

Lucia put the cushion over her head. "I don't want to hear it."

"You should listen," Aretha came beside her, "Ace wants to know if you want to be cheered up. He could drive you somewhere, and then you can take some pictures. Don't you have that calendar thing to do for the supermarket?"

"I don't want to have anything to do with anything Wiley ever again." Lucia sobbed, "Guy has ripped out my heart and trampled on it and then threw pepper and salt on it and chopped it up and fed it to sharks."

"My goodness," Aretha muttered, "this Guy thing went deeper than I thought. You really believed he was perfect, didn't you?"

"Perfect for me," Lucia took the cushion off her head; her eyes were slightly swollen from crying. "Perfect for me."

"It's always a tragedy when we are disappointed in life." Aretha sighed. "I feel your pain. I know exactly how this feels. That is why I was so insistent that you find somebody else, pretty men like Guy are never faithful."

Lucia couldn't control the sob that came out after her mother said that.

She cried for the rest of the day and was listless for most of the two weeks she spent holed up in her room. When she went back to work, she had lost so much weight her regular clothes couldn't fit.

She was skinny to the point of looking angular.

"Wow, you are taking the modeling thing seriously," Arcadia who was the employee of the month again declared after the monthly meeting."

"Very chic looking Lucia what's your secret?" Novalee butted into the conversation.

"Heartbreak." Lucia glared at her, "don't speak to me, do not look at me, pretend as if I am not here."

"But I can't," Novalee whispered. "What has you so upset?"

"You. Are you dense? You slept with my boyfriend!" Novalee growled, "now leave me alone before I call you names. Hoe comes to mind. Promiscuous too. Man stealer."

"Keep your voice down," Novalee hissed.

"Keep my voice down!" Lucia shouted. "Why Novalee? You don't want anybody to know that you sleep around?"

Novalee walked off hurriedly.

They had been creating a scene. Several persons had been watching and listening with interest.

"Are you guys quarreling over the delicious guy that came here to look for Novalee about a week ago?" Arcadia asked.

"Describe him," Lucia demanded.

"Curly hair, medium brown skin, longer eyelashes than mine. Nova was going on and on about how he is a Wiley, and she would be running this supermarket in the near future."

Lucia's heart sank

"He didn't look that much into her," Arcadia said reassuringly. "Besides, if Nova becomes my boss I am moving to another job."

Lucia went through the rest of the day feeling as if somebody had tied weights to her arms and legs. She was listless. She was making mistakes at the register, charging people more than she should and less in some cases.

Reggie took her off the line at twelve and had her waiting in his office like she was a recalcitrant child that was about to be scolded. She was twiddling her thumbs when he came to sit in front of her.

"Lucia, you are off your game today."

"I er, I feel unwell." Lucia sighed. "Can I get two more weeks?"

Reggie looked her over. "How bad is it?"

"Like terrible." Lucia felt her eyes watering. Her hands shook as she tried to put an errant curl behind her ear.

Reggie nodded. "Done. Remember the doctor's certificate when you come back. I hope you get better soon."

So her gauntness was good for something. Lucia left the supermarket and walked over to Folly and sat down at the side of the sea just staring out at the view.

She didn't know how long she sat there, but her thoughts were not positive. This was what betrayal felt like.

Her phone rang several times; she only picked it up and checked that it wasn't Guy before she answered.

It was Ace.

"Lucia, where are you? I am concerned."

And of course, her stupid tears betrayed her. She started sobbing.

"Where are you?" Ace asked urgently.

"Foll...Folly..." Lucia hiccupped.

She didn't know how long it was before Ace came to sit beside her.

"Giving up a relationship is like a death," he whispered after a while, "you will move on. I am here."

Lucia stared out at sea and then turned to Ace. "They are going to have a beautiful babe...babe...baby. That should have been my baby. Novalee is stealing my life. I love Guy; she doesn't. She is nothing more than a filthy gold digger."

Ace grimaced. "One day this pain will pass, and you won't remember why it was so intense."

He clasped his hand in hers, and she did not resist.

****

She got two paying gigs arranged by Ace she was sure of it. One of them was a baby shoot with the chubbiest, sweetest baby she had ever seen. The other was a wedding at a private villa. The couple she was sure was not going to last, the groom kept hitting on her, offered to come and visit her when his wife was asleep in the night.

Ace picked her up after that gig and grinned at her when she came into the car fuming.

"People are so unfaithful. How can you trust anyone?" Lucia griped. "I mean what does he think commitment means?"

Ace listened to her and smiled. "I would never cheat on you. I mean it. I never cheated in any of my relationships. It's not that hard to be faithful."

"I am never having a relationship again." Lucia huffed. "Men are off limits."

"Maybe you need to take your mind off cheating men and come to dinner with me." Ace glanced at her. "Have you started eating again?"

"A little," Lucia sighed, "my appetite is none existent these days."

"Well, that does it," Ace said turning into another villa. "I have it on good authority that the food at Little Wasp is the best."

"Where do you find these places?" Lucia looked around.

Little Wasp was a garden with a view of the sea and Monkey Island in the distance.

They played reggae versions of popular love songs. The breeze was perfect. The summer was shaping up to be pretty hot. Not many people were at the venue. It was the time between lunch and dinner.

"What do you want to eat?" Ace picked up a menu. "I know they have the best jerk chicken and festival over here."

Lucia wrinkled her nose. "A salad perhaps, their jerk chicken salad seems nice."

After they ordered, Ace relaxed in his chair and looked at her. "You are looking better."

"I am okay." Lucia toyed with her blended fruit punch. "I am getting there. Not seeing Novalee and her smug face has contributed to my peace of mind."

Ace tapped the table, "can I be honest with you?"

Lucia nodded. "That's always welcomed. Especially now."

"I took Novalee to dinner the night you chose Guy over me."

Lucia groaned. "What is her appeal? I don't see it."

"Wait, it wasn't like that." Ace sighed, "she said she had information about you and Guy and I stupidly wanted to know more, so I took her. She did tell me that Guy had hit on her and wasn't the faithful type and that she would seduce him away from you."

Lucia gasped. "What?"

"And I told her to go ahead." Ace inhaled deeply, "seeing you in so much pain now has me thinking that this is a mixed blessing. Novalee is all the names you call her and more but don't you think that in all of this, there is a blessing? You found out about Guy before it is too late. Before you joined your life to his and had to suffer this kind of pain."

Lucia closed her eyes for a minute to absorb all that Ace was saying.

She should be angry at all of them, Ace, Novalee, and Guy but she was feeling strangely numb.

"All I am saying, Lucia, is that you forgive Guy and Novalee and give thanks that you are not deeply caught up in their drama."

Lucia nodded outwardly, but she knew it was easier said than done. She didn't know if she was going to ever forgive Novalee or Guy.

She was duped. This kind of pain took years to heal.

But it did heal. She knew that. Her father's wife forgave him. Ace's father forgave his mother. People forgave each other all the time and moved on with their lives even with a child involved.

And it wasn't as if she was married to Guy or even that they had gone further than kissing. It was just that a part of her felt as if there was a grave injustice that happened and that things were not the way that they should be.

Ace cleared his throat, "Lucia I know this is a lot to ask, but the bishop is inviting us to the engagement party."

Lucia blinked rapidly. "No. Count me out. Not on your life."

"You don't have to stay long," Ace said gently. "Show your face, let those two unfaithful disloyals know that you are not hiding and that you see them for what they are. It might help in the healing process."

"When is it?" Lucia gritted out.

"This Sunday evening at the church hall. The manse is too small. The bishop wants this to be a huge deal and probably to save a little face. He is pretending as if it isn't a rushed affair."

****

Guy was on his way from his St Ann farm when he got the call from the bishop. He hadn't heard from him since that night when he had promised to talk to Lucia.

He answered the phone eagerly. "Did you talk to her? What did she say?"

The bishop chuckled. "She agreed to a party. It will be in the church hall, this Sunday evening, most of the parishioners will be there. Of course, as a guest of honor, I expect you to show up."

"A party?" Guy frowned. "Is this a gratitude thing? I don't want her to feel as if she is under any obligation to throw a party I am not one to give speeches in front of a crowd or anything like that. I just wanted to talk to her in private hash out the way forward. Apologize if I caused her any embarrassment. I heard she was crying when she heard... I want to set things right."

"I know, and I very much respect that," the bishop said, "you are an outstanding young man, Guy. Please believe me when I say the party idea was mine. I thought it would add a nice touch and stop wagging tongues in the neighborhood."

"Okay," Guy murmured. "I didn't think she was a party kind of girl, something I thought we had in common."

The bishop chuckled. "Forgive us. She didn't want the party either. She pleaded with us not to throw it, but her mother and I are determined to do the right thing."

Guy chuckled. "The last time I saw Aretha she called me names."

"Who?" the bishop asked.

"Aretha Gordon," Guy said. "The last time I saw her she was furious. Sent me to talk to Novalee."

"God bless her," the bishop said feelingly, "she is a woman of God's own heart."

Guy hung up the phone a smile on his face. He would want to see Lucia before the party, but unfortunately, he had to head to his other farm. Sunday was perfect though. He would ask which one of his brothers would be available; they were all interested in the outcome of his freeze-out by Lucia.

They would be relieved to know that her feelings had thawed out.

He dialed her number, and she didn't pick up. He texted her instead. *I am happy you have forgiven me, see you Sunday at the party.*

Chapter Twenty Two

"**W**hy on earth is Novalee getting married to Guy again?" Earl asked plaintively. Lucia had changed about five times already and was rummaging through her clothes looking for her pretty pink dress with the white hearts.

"Because she is pregnant." Lucia huffed. "She stole my Guy and trapped him with her baby and while that is despicable Guy is not without blame. He had me convinced that he was the faithful type and that what we had was enough. I guess I was wrong."

Earl sat down hard in the chair in her room, which was filled with clothes.

"She does get around doesn't she?"

"Yes," Lucia snorted. "You can stop admiring her and think she is some sort of saint."

"How far along is she?" Earl asked still in his shocked zombie mode voice.

"Probably two months." Lucia found her dress and held it

up. "Does this look better than the one I have on?"

"You look fine in any color," Earl muttered, "Did you say two months?"

"Yes," Lucia glared at him, "can you take your faux shockness and go elsewhere with it. This is an anti Novalee zone."

"When is this party?" Earl asked.

"Three o'clock." Lucia looked up at the clock it was three-thirty. She had no intention of going early or even staying long. Ace was supposed to pick her up, and they were supposed to go to Port Antonio and have ice cream after that.

"Come on," Earl said, "I'll take you."

"Ace is taking me," Lucia said, "I am not staying at this ridiculous party longer than ten minutes."

"But I want to talk to you." Earl looked frazzled.

Lucia frowned at him. "Trouble at work?"

"No." Earl looked terrified. "Work is fine."

"There was a knock on the door, and Lucia looked at her brother. Ace is here. Why don't you come with us?"

Earl shook his head. "No, I'd hate to be the third wheel. I'll drive. We can talk tonight."

Lucia looked at him uncertainly. "You sure?"

"Positive." Earl nodded.

Ace held out a single stem rose when she went on the veranda. "My lady, you look gorgeous as usual."

Lucia smiled. "So do you. You look gorgeous. Your eyes are really something. I call them come-hither-eyes."

And she meant it. He was dressed semi-casually in jeans and a polo shirt. He was tall and dark and handsome with limpid Wiley-esque eyes.

The thought came to her that but maybe she could settle for him sometime in the future if he stuck around through her seesawing emotions. And then one day she wouldn't miss Guy anymore, and he would do. But that was one day, far, far, far in the future. She was still too raw from Guy's deception.

"Have you ever wondered why your eyes look a bit like the Wiley's?" Lucia asked cheekily.

"What?" Ace asked. "My eyes don't look anything like the Wiley's. The grief over losing Guy has you blind."

"No," Lucia chuckled, "am I not Saint Lucia the patron saint of blindness? I can see clearly that you have a bit of the Wiley's about you."

"You remember the patron saint thing?" Ace smiled.

"Yes," Lucia nodded. "I also met all of Guy's brothers when I was in Kingston, and they all had it, the eyes. Some more pronounced than some. And you can't deny that Micky Wiley has it."

Ace was shaking his head. "Oh Lucia, you are far off."

"Ask your mother," Lucia said defiantly. "He was the gardener and around when you were conceived. I watch the law shows; they call it reasonable doubt."

She had made up her mind to tattle on Celia Jackson. Every child deserved to know who their father is.

****

"We are late," Myrtle muttered, "you are late to your own party."

"Blame it on Micky." Guy looked across at his uncle who was glaring at him mutinously.

"This is a brainwashing institution. I don't like going to brainwashing places."

Myrtle chortled. "We are going to a party, you idiot, not to hear a sermon."

Micky hissed. "If they force me to do anything I am out

of there."

Guy chuckled and looked around at the parking lot. There were few cars, many people in the valley did not drive.

However, Guy's family had come out en masse to the party. One by one his brothers pulled up beside him and parked their vehicles.

Most of them had their wives with them except Saint.

Lucia was in for a treat.

However, something was not right. Lucia was a late arrival. She entered the church hall arm in arm with Ace Jackson a little after he drove up.

When he entered the church hall, he saw Novalee sitting at the front of the church hall with a crown on her head. She looked miserable.

Most of the small congregation was there. He recognized many of the faces. The bishop's wife nodded happily when she saw him.

"You have to sit up top, beside Novalee," Mrs. Rochester said helpfully. "And here," She gave him a crown.

Guy took the paper hat bemusement written all over him.

The place was transformed into a banquet hall like atmosphere.

He spotted Lucia at the back her arms folded; she was glaring at him.

"Wait a minute," he tried to make his way over to her.

The bishop intercepted him. "There you are, dear son."

"Son?" Guy's eyebrows almost leaped into his hairline.

"Bishop, what is going on?" He asked above the buzz of conversation.

"You are late; we should begin," The bishop said. "Let's go to the front."

"No." Guy shook his head, "Lucia is in the back."

"What does Lucia have to do with this?" the bishop asked

bewildered.

"She has been giving me the cold shoulder; you said you would talk to her and throw this party because of the Farm Help Society thing."

"What?" the bishop shook his head a little, "Guy you are not making sense."

"I am not making any sense," Guy said a little bit too loudly, "you are not making any sense bishop. Who is this party for?"

"You and Novalee," the bishop hissed, "because of the event, you know. She is two months along. You agreed to this."

"She is two months along where?" Guy fully paid up member of Mensa, the Canadian chapter, asked without blinking.

"She is pregnant!" The bishop said exasperatedly. "You got my daughter pregnant, and now you are pretending that you don't know what this is about?"

The hall was silent.

Guy looked across at Novalee who was inspecting her fingernail with avid interest.

"I have never touched Novalee, not sexually. How would I get her pregnant?"

"I told you it wasn't him," Novalee sobbed from the front.

"Is it mine?" Earl asked weakly from behind Guy, "Lucia said you were two months along?"

Guy looked across at Lucia who was standing with her mouth half opened. It was the expression on most people's faces, except Aretha's. She looked like she was about to faint.

"It is yours, Earl," Novalee admitted in the shocked silence.

"So why on earth did you say it was Guy's?" Earl asked the question that was on everyone's lips.

"I figured out that he was the Farm Help Society and that he was the one who was helping your family. He bought all of those nice clothes for Lucia. I just thought that he would be charitable to me too, I really liked Lucia's Jimmy Choo shoes."

Guy heard a chuckle he didn't have to look behind him to know it was Shawn.

"Sorry about this Bishop." Guy placed his hand on the bishop's shoulders. "I think we were talking about two different things in our conversations."

He walked outside, his family followed.

Jordan was holding up Shawn who was bent over in convulsive laughter.

"Jimmy Choo shoes," Shawn squealed. "She wanted Jimmy Choo shoes."

"So she was going to give the other man's kid to you," Micky muttered angrily, "that's a low down thing to do. I am going to walk it back home. I tell you about these church people, crazy!"

"No, I'll take you." Ace said behind them. "Maybe we can discuss this injustice some more."

"We can take the party up to the house," Myrtle said to no one in particular. "I had cooked up a storm knowing that you all were coming."

"Did you do potato pudding?" Sheryl asked eagerly.

"It is nice and hot," Myrtle answered. "Just removed it from the oven."

Sheryl squeezed him on the arm. "Love always wins, Guy."

Guy nodded.

"I guess your drama topped mine." Shawn elbowed Guy in the side. "I am beginning to think that drama surrounds you Wiley's and not necessarily the women you love. If I were in Lucia's Jimmy Choo shoes and found out that you knocked up my best friend, there would have been hell to pay. Think about that before you get angry with her."

Guy chuckled. "I will."

"I would not have just avoided you," Shawn murmured, "oh no, there would have to be a fight."

"Come on," Jordan hugged Shawn to him, "this is my tiger. I keep forgetting to clip her claws."

"Lucia showed great restraint," Shawn said. "I can't wait to hear her side of the story."

They piled into their various cars to head up to Micky's place. Most of the crowd had scattered.

Guy leaned on his car and waited for Lucia. She was in the church hall with her mother and Earl and the bishop and his wife with Novalee standing among them sobbing.

"I am not marrying her." Earl came out of the churchyard with the small group behind him. "I have a girlfriend in St. Ann. Novalee was just a one night stand. It is what it is Bishop. Sorry."

"Earl, you get back here!" Aretha bellowed. "Now!"

Earl shook his head. "Sorry, mom. I am not marrying anyone to save face. Besides, Novalee is not the kind of girl you marry."

"Excuse me, young man." The bishop looked affronted.

"She is easy," Earl said simply, "if I marry her she will leave me for the first man with a nice car that she sees. She betrayed her friend for shoes! I am sorry, but after the kid is born, I am going to have to get a DNA test. I'll start saving up for it. I don't trust Nova."

Earl got in his van and drove away.

The bishop looked like he was going to faint. Novalee's mother looked at them all apologetically and dragged her daughter away with the bishop following behind a dark scowl in his face.

And then there was just him and Lucia and Aretha.

Aretha came over to where he stood. "Guy Wiley, I am sorry. There are no other words to say except, of course, thank you. You bailed out my family and provided for us through the years when we had no help. You have been a true Christian to us. Even when I was badmouthing you, not once did you mention that you were the reason we even had a roof over our head. I cannot for the life of me understand your selflessness. And I will be forever grateful."

Guy cleared his throat; he was getting uncomfortable with Aretha's praise. "I did it because of Lucia. I wanted her to get the best start in life."

"But you went above and beyond the normal not only for her but for all of us." Aretha's lips trembled. "I should have known that no charity would have been so attentive to our every need.

"I have bashed you. I have dragged your name through the mud. I cannot tell you how many times in the past month I have told my daughter to forget you. I cannot tell you how many times while she was grieving about you and Novalee that I encouraged her to move on to Ace Jackson. I am sorry."

"It is okay, Aretha."

"You don't understand, Guy," Aretha wiped the tears streaming down her face. "You have been more faithful to my family, to my children, than any of the father's in their life. You have been like a big brother to Earl and Nate, and you have never made a pass at Lucia."

"I watched how you treated her, and I waited for you to become one of those men, but you never did. This month I called you faithless. I even called you scum and a pig."

"And I forgive you," Guy said softly, "I understand now why you called me that."

"I pushed her to Ace Jackson because he was a doctor..."

Aretha bit her lip. "No other reason. I must be the worst possible mother on this planet. There are plenty of lessons in this day for me, Guy."

Guy nodded. "For me too."

"I am going to walk it home…have a lot of thinking to do." Aretha looked behind at her daughter who was standing away from them. "Sorry, Lucia."

Lucia nodded.

When Aretha exited the church gate, they were alone. Staring at each other over the overgrown grass in the church front yard.

Guy waited for her to speak.

"I went through hell this month." Lucia walked closer to him. "I took two weeks from work; I lost a lot of weight. I thought you were Novalee's baby daddy."

"I went through hell this month too," Guy said. "My girlfriend left my house with my rival, and she told me she never wanted to see me or hear from me again. I was cut off without an explanation."

"You said you had a secret. I heard she was pregnant and she said it was for you."

"Stupid coincidence, I was going to tell you about the Farm Help Society business when you visited the farm." Guy chuckled dryly. "I already told you I never slept with her."

"I was devastated about nothing." Lucia sighed. "Went around like a zombie."

"While Ace Jackson tried to get you on the rebound." Guy folded his arms, "I saw you with him today, arm in arm."

"He was very sympathetic about my situation, very understanding about my predicament. I unloaded a lot on him this month. He is one of the good guys. He will be perfect for someone else."

Guy stepped away from the vehicle and stood close to her. "So are you saying that Ace Jackson is not in the picture?"

"Yes." Lucia swallowed. "And he knows it. See, he left with Micky. He knows there is no use sticking around. I kind of told him that he was a Wiley. Well, I strongly hinted.

"Mmmph." Guy grunted. "You just opened a can of worms."

"I know, but some secrets are not meant to be kept, like this Novalee pregnancy nonsense. For the life of me, I can't imagine how she thought that she could get away with this. She brought down unnecessary humiliation on herself. I almost feel sorry for her. Sorry enough to give her all of my shoes."

Guy chuckled. "I like that about you, you have a forgiving spirit."

"Only because you are not the father..." Lucia grimaced. "The things I thought about her are not fit to be brought up."

"It's good that you are so forgiving," Guy mused, "because you will always have Novalee in your life if it turns out that she is carrying your brother's child."

"I know." Lucia grimaced. "Lucky me."

"You aren't mad at me that I am the Farm Help Society?" Guy asked.

"No." Lucia chuckled. "What kind of fool would be mad about that? I am grateful. And it makes a lot of sense now. I am thinking thank you is inadequate, they are just words. But, I am going to say it anyway. Thank you, Guy."

"You aren't feeling obligatory feelings of gratitude toward me, are you?" Guy asked cautiously.

"I am not grateful enough to have a relationship with you just because of your generosity or because you are rich." Lucia chuckled. "I am very grateful though, but I don't love you because of things. I think I would love you even if you weren't Guy Wiley certified genius and wealthy farmer who drives a slightly better car than Suzy."

"You are calling my high-end vehicle slightly better than Suzy?" Guy laughed.

"I don't care what you drive." Lucia smiled. "As long as you are in the vehicle with me."

" I think when we get married I'll have to take you around a bit. You deserve some adventure in your life."

"I think I have had enough adventure for now," Lucia murmured. "I am sorry I didn't trust you about the Novalee thing. I could have spared myself a month's worth of tears."

Guy cupped her chin in his hands and stared at her solemnly. "I promise never to be unfaithful. I am not just saying this, you know. I know the results; you forget my parents' convoluted history?"

"Nah," Lucia said solemnly. "I promise to be faithful too, you know my history, faithfulness goes both ways."

"And communication," Guy added, "we have to always communicate. Promise me."

"I promise," Lucia said solemnly.

"Come here," Guy whispered.

"Where?" Lucia whispered back.

"Closer." Guy bent his head until their nose were touching. "These past weeks have shown me that I don't want many more weeks as a single man and that you Lucia should not be far out of my sight."

Lucia smiled. "So what are you suggesting?"

"A wedding right here in the valleys at sunset surrounded by the scent of jasmines and lots of light," Guy whispered.

"That sounds gorgeous," Lucia leaned in to kiss him. "It sounds perfect actually. I always knew you were perfect for me, Guy. You are the perfect Guy."

Author's Notes

Dear Reader,

Thank you for reading **The Perfect Guy**. It was a delight to write. You will see some of these characters again.

Guy was pretty perfect, but I must admit, Ace is not far off in my opinion. I am not about to let him go; he will have his own book in the The Jackson Brothers series. It will be a trilogy, with his other brothers, Deuce and Trey.

As for the Wiley brothers, Saint's story: **Patience of a Saint** is next; an excerpt is on the next page.

As usual, thank you for reading my work. Don't forget to leave a **review** on The Perfect Guy. Reviews are much appreciated.

Thanks again. All the best,

Brenda

**Here is an excerpt from Patience of a Saint
(Wiley Brothers Book 5)**

"Are you coming to the wedding?" Saint leaned on the door to the guest bedroom where Sandrene was lounging on the bed in a state of undress. She was sending a text and didn't immediately respond.

When she deigned to lift her head, there was a frown between her eyes as if she had forgotten the question and had to recall what he asked.

"Why, is it today?"

"No." Saint tried not to snarl, but some of it transferred to his voice. "The wedding is Sunday. We are having all weekend celebrations. Mostly everyone is in Portland already; Case is driving over with us if you are coming."

"I have events booked all weekend at the restaurant." Sandrene shrugged. "Guy's wedding completely slipped my mind. It's not as if your family will miss me there. They hate when I am around. They hate me!"

Saint nodded. "I see."

"That was a loaded I see." Sandrene placed her hands on her hips and turned to him quirking one shapely eyebrow. "So you think I am overreacting?"

"No," Saint shook his head, "They can't stand the new you. They liked you very well before you started acting like a..." Saint sighed. "I do not want to argue today. I am all out. This whole thing is draining. Besides, I am determined to be in a good mood starting today. This is a happy occasion for my family."

"So since you are determined not to feel miserable." Sandrene winked at him, "want to do a quickie while the bed is still warm?"

"Not interested." Saint ran his fingers through his hair in frustration. "Sandrene, it has been four months. Four long months of you acting like a jerk. You threatened to move out last month, and I had no issue with that. Why don't you do it before I get back from Portland? I can't do this anymore."

Sandrene gasped and placed a hand over her breast. "Oh Saint. I thought you would have some patience with me. I am trying here."

"No, you are not," Saint growled. "You changed and not for the better. I can't take this anymore."

"So you are just giving up on our marriage?" Sandrene purred loosening her silky robe and standing before him, in all her shapely glory. "Four years of marriage, down the drain just like that?"

Saint was not moved. There was something wrong with his libido when it came to his wife.

It was the same body, more or less, she had turned into a gym fanatic, and her hourglass figure was honed to perfection. In the past, just one glimpse of her would drive him crazy but not today.

In the past, just the hint of her taking off her clothes would be enough for him to tumble her down on the bed and he would be hard pressed to leave.

In the past, he wouldn't be looking her up and down dispassionately, and unmoved. It was puzzling him.

It was the same come-hither smile on cherry red lips that needed no lipstick to enhance the bow-shaped pout. The same deep bronze skin that had its own glow from top to bottom.

They had married early, he had just been twenty-four years old and she twenty, and he had genuinely thought at the time that he would love her forever. He had never been as attracted to any woman as he had been to her. It hadn't been just lust either. It had been a deep abiding certainty that she was the woman for him.

He couldn't imagine a time when he wouldn't be attracted to her. Sandrene had always had a lightning effect on his libido. Just a smile was enough to turn him on.

But now he found himself glowering in resentment.

"Put your clothes back on; I am serious, I want you gone!"

She shrugged back into her sheer nightgown. "Okay, your loss. I gave you a shot at me for old times sakes. Maybe we could have made a go at this marriage but you for some reason are acting like a beast. I can only assume that you are cheating on me." She sat down at the dressing table and looked at him dispassionately. "I knew this day would come. There is no way you wouldn't succumb to one of those women throwing themselves at you."

Saint groaned out loud. "Sandrene, this is just one example of how different you've been. In the five years since we have been together, you have never accused me of that. You have always known that you were enough.

"We had the kind of sex life that people only dreamed about. There has never been anybody else for either of us. And we loved it that way. We had none of the messy crap from previous relationships or jealous baggage."

Sandrene looked at him sharply. "I was your first? That's crazy! You are so handsome and so many women..."

"That's it," Saint moved away from the door. "It's either you had a personality transplant or a memory block. Were you in an accident that I don't know about and hit your head? I need to know."

Sandrene stopped brushing her cap of curls and put down the brush contemplatively. "I haven't had an accident."

Saint looked at her regretfully, "I think we need the space don't you think? We can't go on this way."

Sandrene nodded. "Yes... er... I think we do need some distance."

Then she breathed out and looked at him with a glint in her eye. "I got married too young. I want to be with other people, see what it's like.

"My life up to now has been a drudge. I hate living here in your Wiley Complex. I hate the other wives. I hate your brothers you are all like a hive mind, thinking and acting like you are all some kind of goodie two shoes.

"I hate their wives and girlfriends. I hate your church. I hate everything about this sorry life, and I want out."

She gave him a defiant look. "I thought it would have been different. Sorry."

Saint didn't respond, every single hate that she just spewed felt as if they nailed him to the floor. He could remember a time when all of those words would have been filled with love instead.

Sandrene had loved living in the complex. She got along well with his brothers, she, Shawn, Sheryl, and Aisha had developed friendships. Sandrene loved the community ministries at church, especially the street feeding program, she didn't mind going out into all types of weather to help starving people. She used to be kind to a fault to strangers, to her family and even her messed up twin sister who didn't get along with anybody for long. He used to think that Sandrene got all the good and Grace Ann got all the evil. Now he was rethinking that.

"Excuse me," she brushed past him and headed to the wall closet where they kept the suitcases.

That was the closest that they had come in four months. After the initial weeks of him being puzzlingly unresponsive to her. They had slept in separate rooms.

Saint looked at her as she grabbed the bags throwing

them unceremoniously in the hallway in a un-Sandrenelike manner.

Something wasn't right with her. A woman didn't go from loving, attentive and sweet to a harpy who hated everything, without some underlying condition. Maybe somebody messed with her brain in her sleep.

He squashed the thought. His explanations for the new Sandrene had gotten wackier by the day; he had resorted to using science fiction for some answers. The brain switch was his latest theory. He had already considered the AI replacement theory.

Saint was swimming in a quagmire of ridiculousness, and he couldn't help it. He had done the pragmatic thing and used up all the private investigators at his disposal. He had tested her DNA against the DNA he had of her on file, and it came back with an exact match.

So it was her, Sandrene, his wife, not some alien replacement but deep in his heart he was still stumped.

How could she change so thoroughly? He had even had fanciful thoughts that this was Gracie instead of Sandrene, but he had clearly heard Sandrene having a conversation with Gracie a week ago about her lovely time in St. Vincent.

"How is Gracie?" he asked cautiously. He didn't want to give away any of his fanciful suspicions.

"She is good." Sandrene looked up at him. "She is contemplating getting married to Roberto."

"When is she coming home to help you out at the restaurant?" Saint raised an eyebrow.

Overwork and stress could be causing her personality change. He was grasping at straws.

Her parents had gone to Australia to help with their son's Jamaican restaurant franchise; Gracie was gone to St. Vincent to be with Roberto. The Waterfalls restaurant was

Sandrene's sole responsibility. It was a popular restaurant with many high-end clients, and they always had an event going. Sandrene had to simultaneously plan events and see to the day to day running of the restaurant.

"In a month." Sandrene glanced at him balefully. "She said that last month, she is so over the moon happy with Roberto, I have no idea if she means it. I am going to have to hire a manager. Mom and Dad are not in a hurry to come back either."

Saint nodded. "That would be a good idea, at least you could get the help."

"But I'll be out of here. As you have wanted for a long time. Have you ever thought that you are the problem?" Sandrene asked, a hint of vulnerability in her voice. "I mentioned moving out because I wanted to know what you would say. You jumped on the idea so quickly."

And he still thought it was best. Saint didn't bother to deny it. "We need some space."

"Well, I'll be at Gracie's apartment." Sandrene huffed, passing him with the bags and heading to the guest room.

Then she stopped at the door and glared at him. "You have my permission to see other people. Live a little, sow those wild oats you never got to sow. Take a mistress or two or ten. I don't care."

Saint leaned on the wall and laughed humorlessly. "You don't care because you'll be doing the same?"

"Oh yes," Sandrene smacked her lips. "Definitely! I need to live a little myself."

Saint shrugged. "Well, you are going to have to curtail that while we are still married to each other. I am a stickler for the marriage vows. I take my vows seriously. You vowed to forsake all others, and while you are married to me, you are going to do just that!"

"What are you going to do? Watch me around the clock?" Sandrene sneered.

"Oh yes," Saint nodded. "Twenty four hours surveillance and you won't even know where my men are and who they are, so you cannot hide!"

"Well, then I am going to divorce you," Sandrene raged, "as soon as I can."

"Fine!" Saint snarled back. "You won't get any argument from me."

OTHER BOOKS BY BRENDA BARRETT

Wiley Brothers Series

Between Brothers (Book 0) - The beginning of the Wiley brothers saga, Joseph Wiley's unconventional family life may prove to be fatal to some members of the family.

For Pete's Sake (Book 1) - Preston has a run in with a child named Pete who claims that he is the grandson of their former housekeeper Pamela Stone.

Crossing Jordan (Book 2) - Jordan is miffed when Shawn takes her new fiancé to Jamaica and insists that he be man of honor at their wedding.

Fire and Walter (Book 3) - Walter's past came rushing to greet him shortly after his appointment as church elder. The new pastor was his childhood molestor, his wife was his ex from college and her cousin was the girl who got away. Walter had a lot of decisions to make.

The Perfect Guy (Book 4) - After a patient five years waiting for Lucia, Guy had his work cut out for him to prove himself worthy of her affections. He had played the part of poor farmer for too long and now he had competition in the form of the handsome doctor Ace Jackson.

The Patience of A Saint (Book 5) - Something was wrong with Saint's wife Sandrene. It didn't take a genius to see that she was changed beyond all recognition. Saint had to get to the bottom of it, before it was too late for them to salvage anything from the relationship.

A Case of Love (Book 6)- After a concert, Case is offered a girl to buy. Her fate was in his hands. He could keep her or leave her to the mercy of her evil family.

Resetter Series

Never Too Late (Book 1)- Addi finds out she is a resetter and goes back to the summer of 92 to change her family's lives.

Never Say Never (Book 2)- Skyler's handsome college lecturer, who happens to be her neighbor, has a 't' in his palms. Should she tell him the significance of it. If she does, would he believe her?

Now or Never (Book 3)- Ten years later Addi and Randy meet again at Randy's engagement party. Why is it that the chemistry between them was still so potent? Can they ever have a future together? Would Randy choose her this time around?

Almost Never (Book 4)- Tech genius Joshua Porter had all but given up on love. He then meets Portia, an inmate at the female penitentiary and his life takes a turn for the adventurous.

The Scarlett Family Series

Scarlett Baby (Book 1)- When the head of the Scarlett family died, Yuri had to return home to Treasure Beach for the funeral. What he didn't count on was seeing Marla, his childhood sweetheart and his best friend's wife. And when emotions overwhelm them and a few months later Marla is pregnant, Yuri wants the impossible: his best friend's wife and the baby they made together...

Scarlett Sinner (Book 2)- Pastor Troy Scarlett realizes the hard way that some sins are bound to be revealed, like the child that he had out of wedlock with his wife's mortal enemy from college. His wife Chelsea was not happy with the status quo. She was not taking care of the son of the woman she had so despised from college. And she could not get over the deep betrayal that she felt from her husband's indiscretion.

Scarlett Secret (Book 3)- Terri Scarlett had a soft spot for her friend, Lola. She was funny and sweet and they looked remarkably alike. But when Lola's Arab prince demands his bride, Terri foolishly exchange places with her friend and they meet up on a world of trouble.

Scarlett Love (Book 4)- Slater always looked forward to delivering packages to the law firm where he could get a glimpse of the stunning female lawyer, Amoy Gardener. Unfortunately, for Slater a woman like Amoy would not take him seriously, especially when she found out that he could not read!

Scarlett Promise (Book 5)- Driven by desperation Lisa Barclay decides to make some extra money by prostituting herself after being kicked out in the streets. Her first customer turns out to be a popular government senator and then to her horror he dies...

Scarlett Bride (Book 6)- When Oliver Scarlett's missionary work in the Congo region was coming to an end, he had a decision to make, marry Ashaki Azanga and save her from being the fourth wife to the chief of the village or leave her to her fate and get on with his life...

Scarlett Heart (Book 7)- After receiving a heart transplant shy librarian Noah Scarlett started to take on character traits that were unlike him and he kept dreaming of a girl named Cassandra Green...

Rebound Series

On The Rebound- For Better or Worse, Brandon vowed to stay with Ashley, but when worse got too much he moved out and met Nadine. For the first time in years he felt happy, but then Ashley remembered her wedding vows...

On The Rebound 2- Ashley reinvented herself and was now a first lady in a country church in Primrose Hill, but her obsessed ex friend Regina showed up and started digging into the lives of the saints at church. Somebody didn't like Regina's digging. Someone had secrets that were shocking enough to kill for...

Magnolia Sisters

Dear Mystery Guy (Book 1)- Della Gold details her life in a journal dedicated to a mystery guy. But when fascination turns into obsession she finds herself wanting to learn even more about him but in her pursuit of the mystery guy she begins to learn more about herself...

Bad Girl Blues (Book 2)- Brigid Manderson wanted to go to med school but for the time being she was an escort working for her mother, an ex-prostitute. When her latest customer offers her the opportunity of a lifetime would she take it? Or would she choose the harder path and uncertain love with a Christian guy?

Her Mistaken Dreams (Book 3)- Caitlin Denvers dream guy had serious issues. He has a dead wife in his past and he was the main suspect in her murder. Did he really do it? Or did Caitlin for the first time have a mistaken dream?

Just Like Yesterday (Book 4)- Hazel Brown lost six months of memory including the summer that she conceived her son, and had no idea who his father could be. Now that she had the means to fight to get him back from the Deckers, she finds out that the handsome Curtis Decker is willing to share her son with her after all.

New Song Series

Going Solo (Book 1)- Carson Bell, had a lovely voice, a heart of gold, and was no slouch in the looks department. So why did Alice abandon him and their daughter? What did she want after ten years of silence?

Duet on Fire (Book 2)- Ian and Ruby had problems trying to conceive a child. If that wasn't enough, her ex-lover the current pastor of their church wants her back...

Tangled Chords (Book 3)- Xavier Bell, the poor, ugly duckling has made it rich and his looks have been incredibly improved too. Farrah Knight, hotel heiress had cruelly rejected him in the past but now she needed help. Could Xavier forgive and forget?

Broken Harmony(Book 4)- Aaron Lee, wanted the top job in his family company but he had a moral clause to consider just when Alka, his married ex-girlfriend walks back into his life.

A Past Refrain (Book 5)- Jayce had issues with forgetting Haley Greenwald even though he had a new woman in his life. Will he ever be able to shake his love for Haley?

Perfect Melody (Book 6)- Logan Moore had the perfect wife, Melody but his secretary Sabrina was hell bent on breaking up the family. Sabrina wanted Logan whatever the cost and she had a secret about Melody, that could shatter Melody's image to everyone.

The Bancroft Family Series

Homely Girl (Book 0) - April and Taj were opposites in so many ways. He was the cute, athletic boy that everybody wanted to be friends with. She was the overweight, shy, and withdrawn girl. Do April and Taj have a love that can last a lifetime? Or will time and separate paths rip them apart?

Saving Face (Book 1) - Mount Faith University drama begins with a dead president and several suspects including the president in waiting Ryan Bancroft.

Tattered Tiara (Book 2) - Micah Bancroft is targeted by femme fatale Deidra Durkheim. There are also several rape cases to be solved.

Private Dancer (Book 3) Adrian Bancroft was gutted when he returned to Jamaica and found out that his first and only love Cathy Taylor was a stripper and was literally owned by the menacing drug lord, Nanjo Jones.

***Goodbye Lonely (Book 4)* -** Kylie Bancroft was shy and had to resort to going to confidence classes. How could she win the love of Gareth Beecher, her faculty adviser, a man with a jealous ex-wife in his past and a current mystery surrounding a hand found in his garden?

***Practice Run (Book 5)* -** Marcus Bancroft had many reasons to avoid Mount Faith but Deidra Durkheim was not one of them. Unfortunately, on one of his visits he was the victim of a deliberate hit and run.

***Sense of Rumor (Book 6)* -** Arnella Bancroft was the wild, passionate Bancroft, the creative loner who didn't mind living dangerously; but when a terrible thing happened to her at her friend Tracy's party, it changed her. She found that courting rumors can be devastating and that only the truth could set her free.

***A Younger Man (Book 7)*-** Pastor Vanley Bancroft loved Anita Parkinson despite their fifteen-year age gap, but Anita had a secret, one that she could not reveal to Vanley. To tell him would change his feelings toward her, or force him to give up the ministry that he loved so much.

***Just To See Her (Book 8)*-** Jessica Bancroft had the opportunity to meet her fantasy guy Khaled, he was finally coming to Mount Faith but she had feelings for Clay Reid, a guy who had all the qualities she was looking for. Who would she choose and what about the weird fascination

Khaled had for Clay?

The Three Rivers Series

Private Sins (Book 1)- Kelly, the first lady at Three Rivers Church was pregnant for the first elder of her church. Could she keep the secret from her husband and pretend that all was well?

Loving Mr. Wright (Book 2)- Erica saw one last opportunity to ditch her single life when Caleb Wright appeared in her town. He was perfect for her, but what was he hiding?

Unholy Matrimony (Book 3) - Phoebe had a problem, she was poor and unhappy. Her solution to marry a rich man was derailed along the way with her feelings for Charles Black, the poor guy next door.

If It Ain't Broke (Book 4)- Chris Donahue wanted a place in his child's life. Pinky Black just wanted his love. She also wanted him to forget his obsession with Kelly and love her. That shouldn't be so hard? Should it?

Contemporary Romance/Drama

After The End--Torn between two lovers. Colleen married her high school sweetheart, Isaiah, hoping that they would live happily ever after but life intruded and Isaiah disappeared at sea. She found work with the rich and handsome, Enrique Lopez, as a housekeeper and realized that she couldn't keep him at arms length...

Love Triangle: Three Sides To The Story- George, the husband, Marie, the wife and Karen-the mistress. They all get to tell their side of the story.

The Preacher And The Prostitute - Prostitution and the clergy don't mix. Tell that to ex-prostitute, Maribel, who finds herself in love with the Pastor at her church. Can an ex-prostitute and a pastor have a future together?

New Beginnings - Inner city girl Geneva was offered an opportunity of a lifetime when she found out that her 'real' father was a very wealthy man. Her decision to live uptown meant that she had to leave Froggie, her 'ghetto don,' behind. She also found herself battling with her stepmother and battling her emotions for Justin, a suave up-towner.

Full Circle- After graduating from university, Diana wanted to return to Jamaica to find her siblings. What she didn't foresee was that she would meet Robert Cassidy and that both their pasts would be intertwined, and that disturbing questions would pop up about their parentage, just when they were getting close.

Historical Fiction/Romance

The Empty Hammock- Workaholic, Ana Mendez, fell asleep in a hammock and woke up in the year 1494. It was the time of the Tainos, a time when life seemed simpler, but Ana knew that all of that was about to change.

The Pull Of Freedom- Even in bondage the people, freshly arrived from Africa, considered themselves free. Led by Nanny and Cudjoe the slaves escaped the Simmonds' plantation and went in different directions to forge their destiny in the new country called Jamaica.

Jamaican Comedy (Material contains Jamaican dialect)

Di Taxi Ride And Other Stories- Di Taxi Ride and Other Stories is a collection of twelve witty and fast paced short stories. Each story tells of a unique slice of Jamaican life.